BEAUTY &
PERSPECTIVE

JEREMIAH COBRA

ISBN 978-1-977-06511-7

To my mother, my sisters, and my brother

Table of Contents

A Draft of My Soul

After the day has worn away at my house, its weathering storms eroding and chipping the paint to form furrows by the attic, creases about the corners of the windows, and streaks like contended margins around my door, which now creaks whenever I admit friends– and strangers;

After the laughter and curses settle in echoes that ring down the halls, caressing and scouring these walls, and once the memory of each love and each feud has marked its indelible fingerprints upon the woodwork and thresholds;

After these windows shield my soul from the tears that rain violently outdoors but keep the sunshine out as well; before the shades are drawn, I welcome the luminance of the moon in quiet solitude. And, I write.

I write to draft my soul into existence, each word forming a foundation, each stanza and paragraph becoming the scaffolding, each poem and story erecting a self-made self made splendidly to withstand the storms outdoors.

And, I can write a fortress. I can draft the outlines to a house with fortified doors and brick walls beyond which strangers are forbidden and curses die in the halls.

Or I can write a mansion. I can make the windows a bit larger with hinges that swing and thresholds that are inviting. I can welcome the sunshine after the storms, the laughter with the curses. Perhaps I should. I write to make sense of a day that would otherwise wear me away.

I exist to write, but also it seems I write to exist, for I cannot live without these words.

Tragedy to Triumph

I was sleeping on pissy mattresses,
Mama weeping and asking if
God was meaning to cast us
Among the thieving and blasphemous.

Daddy gave us beatings; the ashes
Mixed with the bleeding, the lashes
Gave me a reason to bask
Among all the demons,

Till at last I could not fathom
Another ass whipping
Nor be trapped in a perpetual baptism.

So, I'm never giving in,
Fighting until my ending is
Better than my beginning 'cause
That's the meaning of living.

Yeah daddy, he beat the children,
And mama, she kept the kitchen,
But all her preaching and singing
They weren't healing his sickness.

They were concealing his wickedness.
Drunken drug addictions
Were hidden by benedictions

I'm more than a living witness.

A victim from birth, conflicted
But my conviction
Was not to be afflicted
By the sickness I lived with.

So, I'm never giving in,
Fighting until my ending is
Better than my beginning 'cause
That's the meaning of living.

So, next were the homeless shelters
The second story of hell is
The floor where all of the skeletons
Slept with beggars and felons, and

Yet the story gets better when
Words became my medicine
I learned my letters and
A whole heaven lay out ahead of them.

I could see past the pain and wrath
I aimed to last 'til flames were ash,
When it would rain at last.

So, I'm never giving in.
Fighting until my ending is
Better than my beginning 'cause

That's the meaning of living.

I sojourned the path of Douglass
Resolve of Harriet Tubman
I ventured far from the gutters
Where crimes are often unpunished

I earned my pride with prejudice,
Disregarding the devils
And houses of seven gables
For fables of the benevolent

I read– both Ralphs:
Ralph Ellison and Waldo Emerson,
Hugo, Dumas, and Clemens
Helped raise a Yank from Connecticut.

And, I'm never give in
Fighting until my ending
Is better than my beginning 'cause
That's the meaning of living.

The prologue I did not draft,
But I'll write the remaining chapters
With happily ever afters
And passionate cries and laughter,

For one day, I imagine
The masterpiece will be crafted.

I'll sit amongst all the masters,
And have them ask me what happened.

They'll say, "You made it from birth,
"Afflicted to be a victim.
"How'd eschew the script and
"Preserve all your convictions?"

I'll say, "By never giving in,
"Fighting until my ending was
"Better than my beginning 'cause
"That's the meaning of living."

Before He Used His Father's Gun

"Must I inherit the sins of my forefathers?" Issac wondered aloud. "Must I honor their ideas simply to relive their misery?" He stood alone before the gates of his childhood home. His tears blurred the town of Moriah into a kaleidoscope of flickering street lamps, broken windows, and weed-ridden lawns. He blinked away those tears to see clearly his father's old revolver, his own steady hand that held it, and a childhood scar on the wrist of that hand. There was a day when he trembled to hold this gun. Today was no such day.

He tucked it into the waistband of his jeans and turned toward the house to which he had become a stranger. Long after his father had inherited it, the house's wood panels were rotted, and its blue paint was chipped and grayed. The gate screeched as he pushed it open to walk through the thinly scattered blades of grass, his steps finding only the crumbled vestiges of a once homeward path. By the driveway, he paused to gaze at the rusted sedan that seemed to grow from the weeds and asphalt below it. Once his father's most prized possession, the car sat with its tires saggy and cracked. Its once lustrous paint was peeled and faded to reveal the scarred steel beneath. Its windows were made foggy by many a weathering storm. Its headlights were yellowed like the eyes of a jaded drunkard.

As he turned to the front door, he realized that he did not wish to encounter the void that had grown behind it. He would only find empty rooms in which happiness had been stunted by gloom, and he would only mourn a life that should have but could not have been. He shuddered as he pushed his key into the worn lock and turned the knob. The door was heavy with age, and the thick, dusty air inside flowed like molasses into his nostrils. He took a tentative step past the threshold, and the echo of the creaking floorboard skittered down the darkened halls. For a brief moment, he thought his father might emerge from that darkness with drunken gait and clenched fists. He thought of the gun at his waist, but he did not reach for it.

By the remnant light of dusk, Issac saw that the house had come undone. He stumbled over couch pillows that had been thrown to the floor, and he broke his fall by the old coffee table upon which newspapers and unopened mail lay sprawled. He wandered into the dining room where emptied nips of scotch and vodka told a solemn tale. He found the rotting smell of unwashed dishes swelling from the cavity of the sink in the kitchen. He traversed the barren halls to the dark and dusty stairwell where every step expelled a protest to its dwellers. He swept aside worn clothing and old furniture in his parents' bedroom where the scent of stale smoke wafted about from full ashtrays. He all but held his breath as he searched the closet for a knapsack and some clothing to fill it. Finally, he made his way to the second stairwell leading up to the attic, his old bedroom. It was only as he approached the attic door that he began to feel a bit at ease.

The rusted hinges whined when he pushed the door open, and a heavy and stagnant air poured into the hall. Yet, there was light from the tiny window within, and that light beckoned him away from sullen chambers. Inside, a veil of dust and cobwebs had settled upon all of the furniture, but the order of the room was preserved. An old quilt lay perfectly smooth upon his bed. His wardrobe stood stoically in one corner of the room, and his books were lined neatly on the shelf against the wall that rose to meet the slant of the roof. The faintly sweet musk of an old pine chest emanated from its place at the foot of his bed. He took a deep breath and walked over to it.

When he lifted the cover to the chest, the first thing he saw inside was a small crystalline music box topped by a figurine. A tiny ballerina stood en pointe atop a tiny grand piano. Issac sat on his bed and wound the music box. He watched the ballerina twirl to the sound of his mother's favorite song. Closing his eyes, he easily and vividly envisioned his mother, the once beautiful dancer.

Farah sauntered gracefully about a tidy kitchen filled with the aroma of simmering collards and baking cornbread. She reached down and grabbed her son's tiny hands while humming her song. They danced and jumped about the room, and their cheeks felt as though they would burst from smiles and laughter. Issac admired her cheeks, like tourmaline set aglow by the sun's kisses upon them. As she twirled about the room, her hair waved about and shimmered like raven feathers. Indeed, she seemed to have wings.

"Are we flying?" Issac asked her as they danced, for surely there was no higher aspiration than this joy that both of them took for granted.

But soon, the music box wound down in his hands. The song slowed until the crystalline figure no longer danced but languished. Then, he saw Farah sitting solemnly in the living room, her hair disheveled, her dream deferred, and the corners of her eyes creased by wrinkles of despair. Slowly, a tear trickled along these wrinkles and down her round cheek before landing among spirits glittering in a crystal glass. It was the first time that Issac would remember seeing his mother so stricken by sadness. He was four years old.

"Though he slay me, yet will I have faith in him," she whispered the words softly, perhaps as a psalm to God or perhaps as a prayer for the many fights she would have with Issac's father. Though her whispers were meant to restore her spirits, they sounded to Issac like surrendered feathers fluttering down from her wings. He feared that one day those wings would no longer fly.

The music box froze in Issac's hands, and he heard the subtle rustling of footsteps through dry leaves outside. Someone was approaching the gate. He thought of the gun at his waist, but he did not reach for it. Instead, he calmly placed the music box beside him on his bed, and he reached into the chest again for an old photo. He was five years old in that photo, and the football he held was far too large for his hands. His father was in that photo, too, standing so tall that his forehead had been cropped out. His face remained, however, with eyes darkened by the shadow of his furrowed brow, nose perpetually flared, and mouth drawn slightly downward at its corners. Abram looked stern, angry even, but Issac remembered his father's smile on that autumn morning.

The sun was not yet higher than the trees in their backyard, and it shone through a canopy of crimson, orange, and gold leaves. The air was crisp, and the smell of burning wood wafted about from the chimneys. Issac's hands were chapped from the cold, hard leather that met his palms with each attempt to catch his father's passes. When Issac finally held on to the football, his heart leapt in his chest.

"My boy is gonna be a ball player!" Abram declared with a wide grin. Certainly in that moment, Issac did not want to be anything more. His father had spoken a dream into his soul– a heaven to which he could aspire. If only Abram knew that fathers can speak heaven or hell into existence for their children. Perhaps he would not have given utterance to so much hell.

"It's like everybody in this world wanna take your joy," he echoed words he had heard long ago. "Sometimes, I think they wait for you to start looking for joy. That's when they hunt. Their bait is the food in your mouth and every desire of your heart. That's how they got my pops– turned everything and everyone he loved into a thing to be worked for, a leash to hold him by. Made him work 'til the very end."

"But his heart killed him," Farah said. Abram shot her a menacing but fleeting expression.

"I ain't gonna let nobody have that kind of power over me."

"Sometimes you gotta sacrifice for the people you love," Farah said.

"And I sacrifice plenty!" Abram replied. "Y'all got a hold on me, and they know that. They treat me like a slave 'cause they know as long as I wanna take care of y'all they own me."

"Is that how you see us?" Farah asked, "As bait for someone to control your life?"

"That's just how it is. Everybody eats somebody. That's how you get ahead. I'm the dumbass because I'm just sitting here trying to drink this beer in peace– in my house."

"It ain't gonna be yours for long if you don't get a real job," Farah said.

Her last words felt to Abram like the pull of a chain around his neck, and he slammed the bottle down on the kitchen table in protest. The bottle shattered in his hand, and he howled.

"Aww shit!"

Beer and blood mixed and dripped to the floor. Farah's eyes widened with panic as she looked at the gash in Abram's palm.

"Give it here. I can fix it," she said as she searched frantically for a bandage. When she found a clean one and approached him, he pushed her against the table on his way out the back door. He did not return until just before dawn the next morning.

Issac looked sorrowfully at his father's expression in that photo. He decided that it was not one of sternness or anger but one of pain. Perhaps Abram wished to smile in that photo, in that moment. But his own thoughts kept him from doing so. Issac placed the photo near the music box as he listened to the gate screech open outside. Soon, the front door sounded a deep groan downstairs as it was pushed through the threshold. The familiar, heavy footsteps that trod through the hallway and into the living room made Issac's heart drop into the pit of his stomach.

Thump, thump.

He thought about the gun at his waist, but he did not reach for it. Instead, he thought about the day he got that gun. He was seven years old.

On a harsh, cold winter evening, Abram stumbled drunkenly into the kitchen through the back door and slammed a revolver down on the kitchen counter by the sink.

"What's that?" Farah asked nervously.

"It's a gun, Farah."

"I mean, what is it doing there?"

"It's sitting there."

"You know what I mean. Why did you bring it in here? You told me you would never bring that back in here."

"Don't be questioning what I bring in my house. I'll bring whatever I want in here."

"But it kills people!"

"No, those niggas out there kill people."

"Then keep it out there for them. I ain't never questioned how you get your money, but don't bring that foolishness around me or our son."

"Well, that's my pop's gun; it ain't going nowhere."

"But you know what you did!" she began to whimper. "You told me what you've had to do with that gun."

"And you think I'll do that in here? Who I'mma shoot? You? Our son? You gonna give me a reason? It ain't going nowhere."

"Then we are!" Farah replied and stormed out of the kitchen toward the stairwell.

"Like hell, you are!"

She rushed from the room and he behind her. They entered the hall where he grabbed her firmly by the arm just as she reached the stairwell. He jerked her away from the handrail and grabbed her other arm to hold her still.

"You ain't taking my son nowhere," he said resolutely, "You wanna leave, fine. But you don't take nothing that's mine with you. I done worked too hard for it."

"Let me go!" she said, "You don't own me."

They tussled about in the hallway until he finally released her. She grabbed her coat and headed for the front door.

"Where you gonna go? You just gonna come back again, like you always do. Ain't no better life out there. Ain't no better man—" Abram's voice faded into the winter air and cut abruptly beyond the closing door.

When he was sure that they were both gone, Issac, who had been eavesdropping from the upper staircase, tiptoed downstairs to the kitchen. He was both intrigued and afraid when he saw the menacing gleam of the gun's barrel under the fluorescent light. He slowly walked over to touch the handle. The carving there felt abrasive against his palm, and his arm trembled with the weight of the revolver as he picked it up. It seemed to him that he held a most curious charm. Might it bring good luck or harm? Did it nurture man's nature, or did man's nature nurture it? Did it hold his father spellbound in anger? Had it brought his grandfather bad luck on that day so many years ago? Issac hoped that it might bring him good luck that day, for in that moment he simply wished for his mother to stay.

Opening the back door, Issac carried the gun into the yard. Immediately, he began to shiver from the frosty air and the ice and snow beneath his bare feet. He scurried quickly to a large elm that sat in the middle of the yard. He climbed the tree until he came to an old nook inside which he carefully hid the gun. Then he hurried back into the house and up the stairs to the attic. He left his door open so that he heard when his father crashed drunkenly through the front door. Farah was not with him. Issac's heart pounded as Abram's heavy footsteps thumped through the hallway, and into the kitchen. There was silence for a moment before those heavy footsteps trudged back into the hallway and up the first stairwell.

Thump, thump.

Issac was relieved when he heard the sound of his parents' bedroom door open and close. Only then could he fall asleep.

"Wake up, little nigga," a deep and gravely voice broke Issac's slumber and he was startled to see a broad, shadowy figure perched at the edge of his bed, its features blending like a ghost into the darkness.

"You know where my gun is?"

The pungent smell of alcohol and tobacco ash rose forth from the ghost's throat and settled like a fog upon Issac's pillow. Issac tried to sit up and escape that fog, but a wide hand upon his chest anchored him to the bed.

"No," Issac answered groggily.

"You're lying. I'll ask you again. Where is it?"

The boy's heart pounded against the ghost's hand, and he found that his words were frozen on the back of his tongue. The ghost broke the silence.

"So you just gonna sit in my house and lie to my face? Okay then."

Issac's heart raced as he listened to footsteps fade from the room and down the stairs. When he could no longer hear them, he thought that his own heart had stopped. However, when the footsteps returned, they shook the floor in the halls and stairwell.

Thump, thump.

They resonated in his chest.

Thump, thump. Thump, thump.

Issac looked frantically about the room for someplace to hide.

Thump, thump! Thump, thump!

The familiar jingle of a buckle rang in the air as the shadow, darker than the darkness in the doorway, returned. Issac sprang to his feet when he saw the loop of leather in its hand, and he skittered to the farthest corner of the room where an old desk sat had been built into the wall long ago. The desk had aged with the house and the nails with which it was built had rusted and come loose. Many protruded from a beam of wood that stood separated from one of the desk's legs. Issac sought refuge amidst jagged edges beneath this broken desk, and the ghost wafted after him and settled upon his haunches.

"What you think, boy? That I'm less dangerous without that gun?"

The ghost ducked its head down to peer farther under the desk.

"You think that gun will give you power, but you don't know what I've gone through to keep this house. I'll tell you that much stronger than you have tried to uproot me from this house, but I persist. Like a bad memory. Now where is it? You gonna use it on me boy?"

"I don't know," Issac replied with a quiet, helpless whimper. He felt a strong grip tighten about his collar.

"If you got it, you better use it right now. But don't miss, or your butt is mine."

Issac, feeling as though there was no other way out of this encounter finally cried, "I threw it away!"

At first there was no response. The grip around his collar loosened, and the sound of Issac's breathing swelled in his own ears. He continued.

"Mama didn't want it in here, I thought she would come back if I threw it away."

Still, there was no response, and Issac could hear his own pulse.

Thump, thump. Thump, thump.

Then, a simple response.

"Okay."

Issac thought that he had said enough to make the ghost disappear. But suddenly, it sprang forward and grabbed Issac by the leg. For a brief moment Issac was able to hold tightly to one of the desk legs, but it soon yanked him free. Issac felt lifeless as he was raised to his feet. His right sleeve had become damp and sticky, and when the ghost let go of him, he heard his own cry and the collapsing of his body as a distant echo. The ghost went away and a light suddenly flooded the room. He saw his father, but more so, he saw himself through his father's eyes. He saw a child writhing on the floor and the blood streaming down his wrist and dripping from his fingers. He saw the crimson stripe that had been torn across his wrist. He felt his father's heart crumble.

"No, no, no, no, no..." Abram stammered as he dropped to his knees and used his own hand to stop the bleeding.

"Farah!" he cried as though words alone might bring her home, "Our son!"

He scrambled in a panic to bandage his son's arm, and he sobbed so loudly that Issac briefly forgot about his own pain.

"What have I done? My son! My own blood!"

Issac looked at the scar that had grown with him over the years. How awful that it should always remind him of man in his weakest moment, of man on a day when he could break his own heart? What capacity is there in man to harm that which he holds dear?

"And what about me?" Issac thought with a whisper. "Must I inherit my father's sins?"

Issac could hear his own heart in his chest.

Thump, thump.

It kept pace with the sound of the heavy footsteps filling the lower stairwell.

Thump, thump.

He thought about his father's gun, but he did not reach for it. Not yet. A lump rose in his throat as the footsteps continued past his parents' bedroom and into the upper stairwell to the attic.

Thump, thump. Thump, thump.

Issac could feel the sweat forming on his palms.

Thump, thump! Thump, thump!

Without realizing it, Issac began to slowly creep his hand to his waist. The footsteps grew louder until they were just behind the attic door. Issac heard his father's exhales brushing the wood. A jingling sound rang in the air, and Issac stared at the unmoving doorknob. His heart stopped. Then suddenly, the footsteps turned and retreated. Down the upper stairwell, past the bedroom, down the lower stairwell, through the hallway. Out the front door. Issac sighed with relief as he looked out the attic window to see his father sitting on the hood of the rusted sedan. With slumped shoulders, Abram looked pensively toward the horizon and took sips from a beer bottle. Issac thought that his father looked defeated yet peaceful for once, and he was reminded that no matter how many times his mother threatened to leave, she always returned. She always weathered his storms.

"Is he a bad man?" Issac once asked his mother when he was nine and he found her crying after an argument. As usual, Abram had gone with fervor from the house, and Farah sat on the living room floor with her hair tousled, her blouse torn, and her cheeks flushed.

"No," Farah replied, "Just because some people do bad things don't mean they're bad. He means well. He wants to take care of us, and he's doing it the only way he knows how."

"But he makes you sad," Issac said. "You're so sad, sometimes."

"Well, that's why I have you. You make me happy."

Issac looked at the sadness in his mother's smile, and he knew that he was not enough to quell the angst that his father had given her.

"One day, when you grow up," Farah explained, "you'll see that you must love people in spite of their flaws."

"What if the person you love always hurts you?" Issac asked.

"I don't know. Maybe you have to be strong enough to love them anyway."

From the attic window, Issac tried to look past his father's yellowed, jaded eyes, his grayed beard, and his faded complexion. He tried to envision the man from the picture, the man who was once so proud to watch his young son learn to catch. He tried to see the man whose running stride he tried to match when he was five years old, and he remembered how impossibly fast his father seemed. He remembered a time when he and his father walked through blizzard snows, and he kept falling in his father's deeper footsteps. On that day, when he struggled too long, he would find himself lifted by his father's hands to higher, firmer ground. As he daydreamed, Issac once again saw the long rides in his father's sedan– Abram's prized possession because it was once his father's car, too. Abram taught Issac to love the smell of the gasoline powering the carburetor engine, the soft glow of the lights illuminating the dashboard, and the smooth touch of leather so soft he could sink into it. Abram once promised to teach Issac how to care for that car some day. That day never came, and Issac's daydream became blurred by heartbroken tears.

Vividly, he saw the first time he received a beating from his father. He did not remember what he did wrong, but he remembered the pain. He remembered the dreaded sound of his father's belt buckle jingling outside his door. He remembered the first time he learned to fear his father's anger. He looked at the dagger-shaped scar on his wrist, and he recalled the day he fell out of love with his father. It was their last car ride.

"My pops was tough on me," Abram began as he guided the long sedan down the main street. Issac sat with his eyes fixed upon the world passing outside the window.

"It was good, though. I grew up tough. I learned how to live in the world. No part of the world has changed since he been gone. I'm trying to teach you how to survive in it. You understand?"

Issac nodded, but he did not understand. He simply gazed out the car window and imagined that he was out there running as quickly as the world seemed to pass. He leapt over the people meandering the streets and sidewalks, and he took flight among the leaves and clouds. He stared longingly at the autumn canopies.

Moriah was not a pretty neighborhood. The litter-filled streets, abandoned buildings, and graffiti-ridden walls made for despondent spring rains, grimy summer heat, and bitter winter snows. But Issac did like Moriah in the autumn. The colorful branches of maple and oak leaves arched over the streets and reminded him of a joy that belied the despair prowling the sidewalks every day. Indeed, he preferred to gaze up at the trees, but that day he caught himself looking down at the drunken and drug addicted who wandered about like zombies, the idle men who slouched on corners, and the young girls who pranced about, pretending to be adults.

"You must think I'm some sort of bad guy for you to take my gun, huh?" Abram chuckled as if he were reading Issac's thoughts. "That's alright. You gotta protect your mother. I can respect that. Protect your birthright. But, there's a whole lot worse out here than me. You see me being pissed? That's just me protecting you and your mother. She knows it– she gets it. You think a smile is gonna tell these niggas to back up off me? You gotta let them know with one look that they can't mess with you. You let them see you smiling, and they'll wanna find out why you're smiling– figure out a way to take that smile away from you. Understand?"

They came to a stoplight, and Issac noticed an abandoned building and two men who stood on its doorstep arguing loudly. One of them threateningly raised a bottle cloaked in a paper bag. He shouted a few curses at the other man and brought the bottle down hard upon his head. Issac gasped. Abram chuckled. The light turned green.

As Abram guided the sedan skillfully around two jaywalking teenagers, he continued his lecture.

"Who you think is more foolish, the man who swung or the man who got hit?" he asked.

Issac did not answer.

"Which one you wanna be?" Abram asked.

"Neither."

"Hmph!" Abram snorted. "You gonna be better than both of them, huh?" He removed a cigarette from behind his ear and lit it. Then he took a long draw from it and exhaled a blue cloud against the windshield.

"I used to wanna be better, too," he mumbled past the cigarette balanced between his dry lips, "But you live long enough and learn one thing: there ain't but two kinds of men in this world, and you better learn to be the man that swings first— 'less you wanna be the man who don't swing at all. Can't make it outta here if you dead."

He inhaled more smoke.

"Can't make it outta here, no how."

He exhaled a blue cloud that fogged the windows and stung Issac's eyes. "Deer and hunters. Lots of deer out here. Better make sure you're a hunter."

Issac sat with his head to the sliver of an opening in the window, and he tried to no avail to sneak breaths of the fresher air as it whisked by. He was not sure that his father was wrong, but he would thenceforth spend much of his time contemplating the kind of man he could be.

§   §   §   §

"Ain't no more money to fix it!" the heavy bass of Abram's voice pounded against the walls while the treble of Farah's shrill retorts cut through the air.

"You ain't never got no money to fix nothing!" Farah shouted, "You spend all day out there, and then you come back here with no money for nothing! We need that car, so you find some way to fix it."

"What, I'm s'posed to do? I already owe the man money," Abram replied.

"You *s'pose* to get a job!"

"Damn that! I'm supposed to go let somebody put a chain on my life?"

"No!" Farah yelled. "You're supposed to make sure your son has a life. Make sure he got enough to eat. You supposed to come home at night, and stop making me wonder if you coming home at all. I'm tired of that! I'm tired of praying!"

"Then leave!" Abram cried, "See if you find better out there. You'll see what I been talking about real quick."

Issac sat for a while in the stairwell, his focus oscillating between their bristling voices and his grumbling stomach. Before long, his hunger pangs consumed all of his focus, and he headed out of the house, into a neighborhood that was deceptively still during the afternoon. He walked past the rows of houses until he came to the main street. To the left, he heard the train whistle and rumble as it left the station. To the right, the neighborhood stretched for several blocks. Straight ahead, delicious aromas beckoned him to a corner bakery across the street. He reached into his empty pockets and turned right.

As he walked the street, he encountered all of the familiar sights. At the barbershop, he could hear one of the barbers joking with a patron.

"Now, you know damned well we black folks don't– " the voice chuckled as Issac continued onward. A church with a large sign out front asked him to put his troubles in God's hands. A voice on a car radio sang the evils of money to the rhythmic thumping of bass and drum lines. A man with street-stained skin and ragged clothing begged for change. Issac shrugged, and continued onward.

Finally, Issac arrived at a small house with a large garage and several broken-down cars parked outside. In its driveway, one elegant, expensive sedan glittered in the afternoon sun. He walked to the large garage and ducked under the door to find an old gentleman bent over the hood of a broken coupe.

"Can you teach me how to fix these?" Issac asked. The old gentleman looked up from the hood. He was short and stocky with baggy, grease-stained overalls, peppered gray wool for hair, and a bushy gray beard. He peered over his large spectacles and cleared his throat.

"Ya Abram's boy, eh?"

"Yessir," Issac replied.

"Ya come to bring me da money he still owes me?"

"He doesn't have any money, Mr. Braithwaite."

"Den ya come to tell me when he gon' 'ave da money?" Mr. Brathwaite looked sternly at Issac, his lips pursed tightly and drawn downward, his eyes becoming slits above the wide, glass ovals.

"He isn't going to have it."

"And ya come 'ere to tell me dat, boy?" Mr. Braithwaite huffed incredulously.

"I came here to work," Issac pointed to the broken coupe. "Can you teach me to fix that?"

Mr. Braithwaite peered at him a while longer, as if he were solving a difficult puzzle. Then he chuckled and went back to work on the coupe.

"Well?" Issac asked.

"Ya ain't never drove a car before, 'ave ya?"

"No, sir. I'm fifteen."

"Den, no!"

Issac sighed and turned toward the door. He was not sure where he would go, but he did not want to return home. He was about to duck under the garage door when Mr. Braithwaite spoke again.

"But ya can 'and me dat wrench ova dere."

Issac looked back to see an unsmiling face that was nevertheless wrinkled by benevolent concern. Issac hurried to find the wrench and bring it to Mr. Braithwaite who took it and returned to his work, though not before giving another command.

"And ya can sweep da floors. Da broom is in dat corner," Mr. Braithwaite gestured to a place with an old apron, several greasy rags, and an old, wood-handled broom. Issac took the broom and swept the floors with diligence and gratefulness. He performed several other chores that day, and after the sun set, Mr. Braithwaite approached Issac with a clean rag to wipe his face and hands. Buried in the rag were a few folded bills.

"Ya come back tomorrow afternoon if ya wanna work," Mr. Braithwaite proposed, "Ya show me ya work ethic, and I'll teach ya how to fix cars, eh?"

"Yessir," Issac replied with a smile.

"Ya know, I knew ya grandfather. He was a mean son-of-a-bitch, but he always paid his debts."

"Yessir," Issac nodded.

Mr. Braithwaite peered at Issac's face for something familiar. He frowned with discernment before he nodded at the teenager.

"Go on, den."

Issac walked the street with the bills folded tightly in his fist. However, he remembered his father's words and wore his smile on the inside all the way home.

After a few days of working for Mr. Braithwaite, Issac returned home to find his father sitting at the kitchen table with a cigarette and a glass of whiskey.

"The hell you smiling for?" Abram asked when he saw his son's face, " And where the hell you been?"

"Helping you," Issac replied. Abram furrowed his brow.

"Oh? How'd you do that? You ain't been here?"

"I got a job. I been helping Mr. Braithwaite at his garage down the street."

"And how does that help me?"

"You don't owe him for the car anymore."

"What are you talking about?" Abram raised his voice.

Issac became confused. He had expected his father's smile, and when he didn't see it, Issac felt his own smile fade. He felt his words freeze at the back of his tongue.

Abram stared at his son for a long, silent moment. Then, the screech of his chair against the floor pierced the air as Abram rose quickly to his feet and rushed toward his son. In an instant his hands were gripped tightly to Issac's collar as he pinned him to the wall.

"You did what?" Abram growled.

"I– I wanted to help."

"You don't help me!"

Abram's voice was raspy from smoke, scotch, and rage. He jerked Issac's collar such that the boy's head banged against the wall. The tears welled in Issac's eyes as he felt the whiskey-laced spittle and tobacco-stained breath from his father's mouth upon his face.

"What you gonna be the man of the house, now?" Abram asked, "Because you done gone out and told the whole world that your daddy ain't no man. You gonna feed us now?"

"I can," Issac replied in earnest.

Abram's eyes darted back and forth to scowl into each of his son's eyes. But then his grip on Issac's collar loosened, and he slowly took a step back. Then he released his son and looked around until he remembered where he had left his drink. He grabbed the whiskey bottle as he headed toward the backdoor.

"So you're a sheep, then." Abram said with his back to Issac. "Let them wolves eat you up. Just make sure you're home by supper every day." He opened the door. "And clean up the kitchen before your mama gets home."

When the door slammed closed, Issac stood for a moment with his fists clenched, his breaths rushed, and his heart racing. Then, as if an instinct had seized his body, he stormed out to the backyard to retrieve his father's gun. He slept with it under his pillow that night and kept it in the pine, toy chest thenceforth.

In the months that followed, Issac worked and learned in the evenings with Mr. Braithwaite. Every Friday, Mr. Braithwaite paid him in cash, three-quarters of which Issac would take home and tuck into his mother's cigarette case. The remainder went in a shoebox under his bed. Sometimes, he even brought home groceries.

One day, as they sat at the dining room table eating food that Issac had proudly purchased and prepared for his parents, Issac looked up to see his father looking askance at him.

"You a good deer, ain't you?" Abram goaded his son, "Just let them hunters eat you up, huh?"

"I ain't no deer," Issac said defiantly, "Mr. Braithwaite don't hunt me. He pays me. He teaches me. Maybe I can fix the car, now."

"Better not touch my car," Abram warned.

"Leave him alone, now," Farah said to Abram, but he did not stop.

"Nah, nah, you a deer alright. And you know who I am?"

"I said leave him alone," Farah raised the tone in her voice.

"I'm the hunter in them streets. Nobody messes with me out there," the excitement grew in Abram's voice, "Yeah, I'm the hunter out there and in here, too. And you're a deer."

"I ain't no deer!"

Abram raised a chicken leg from his plate while Issac could feel the blood grow hot about his collar.

"Yeah, you see this here? You know what this is? This is you!" Abram pointed the drumstick at Issac. Then, he took a big, ravenous mouthful of the seared flesh into his mouth.

"They'll eat you up out there, and you're just begging them to do it, huh?"

"That's enough!" Farah shouted.

"Nah, nah he's alright," Abram said, "He's cool. Deer don't do shit, and they damn sure don't say shit. Ain't that right boy?"

Issac had enough. He leapt across the table at his father who caught him in an instant and hurled him to the ground.

"Oh ho!" Abram groaned with facetious trepidation, "You trying to be a hunter, now!"

"Issac, you stop!" Farah shrieked, "Abram, you shut up!"

But neither Issac nor Abram heeded her command. Issac gathered himself and threw his wiry frame at his father who once again caught him and hurled him against the table, sending the food, plates, and silverware tumbling to the ground. Then, Abram grabbed his son by the collar and scruff of his neck and held him up against the wall. Issac gasped and choked as he forced curses out of his mouth and at his father's face.

"Stop!" Farah screamed, "You stop talking to your father that way!" She ran over to pry her son from his father's grip. "And you! Don't do him like your father did you," she pleaded with Abram who ignored her and leaned in closer to his son to hiss the words past his own clenched jaw.

"I'm the hunter in here, you understand? And as long as you live here, I don't care how much money you make, I'll eat you up!"

He released Issac who tumbled to the ground but scrambled quickly to his feet.

"Go up stairs, Issac!" Farah pleaded, "Get out of here!"

His vision blurred by his anger, Issac stumbled through the hall and up the stairs to the attic.

Thump, thump!

When he got to his bedroom, he slammed the door open and hurled the mattress from his bed. He grabbed the revolver that lay there, and he hurried to the stairwell. He froze at the top of the stairs, his hand trembling with the weight of the gun, his breath heavy with fury, and his eyes flooded by tears. However, before he used his father's gun, he dropped to his knees.

"Must I inherit my father's sins?" he uttered as he let the gun fall to his side. "Must I keep his demons?"

Slowly, he crawled to his room and collapsed on his mattress. He placed the gun under his pillow and fell fast asleep.

He awoke to his mother seated beside him, gently stroking his hair.

"My son," she spoke softly.

"Why does he hate me?" Issac asked. Farah chuckled.

"He don't hate you. He's your father."

"He wanted to fight me!" Issac shouted. He tried to sit up, but the soft and calming touch of his mother anchored him to the bed.

"You can't be fighting your father," Farah said. "You gotta let some things he says slide. He don't mean no harm."

"He choked me."

"You swung first! How you gonna win that fight? He been fighting all his life. Even fought his own father. He's too good at it."

She was trying to force humor into her words, but there was too much truth in them.

"His daddy was a hard man. Put your father through hell. But Abram grew up to respect his father's way. He's just trying to teach you how his daddy taught him. Just stay out of his path for a little while. He'll be alright."

"Mama, why are you always sticking up for him?"

"Because love sometimes means sticking up for people even when they're wrong. A boy needs his father, after all. Try to honor him as best as you can, okay?"

Many years later, his mother's words seemed to linger in the stagnant air of the attic, and Issac suddenly longed to open the window and let them fly away into the cool, autumn air. He looked down at his father who continued to sip from the bottle and sit upon the hood of his rusted sedan.

What would he do if I went to him now, Issac thought to himself. Would he embrace me or choke me? Would I let him do either? Issac thought about the gun at his waist, but he did not reach for it. Not yet. Slowly, he moved away from the window and picked up the knapsack. He slung it over his shoulder and headed out of the attic to the upper stairwell. He remembered the last time he performed these exact actions. He was sixteen years old.

He returned home and looked under his bed to find his shoebox missing. Immediately, he stormed downstairs to the living room where his father sat on the sofa.

"Where is it?" he demanded with a wild look in his eyes.

"Where is what?" Abram seemed unconcerned as he watched television.

"My money. It's gone."

"Maybe it's wherever my you threw my daddy's gun," Abram replied.

"You can't take my money!"

"You don't have no money in my house."

Issac looked with bewilderment at his father who spoke without looking away from the television.

"When you get your own house, you can have money and whatever else you want in it. But this is my house. You don't have no money here," Abram continued.

"I pay rent here!" Issac cried, "I buy half the food! I feed myself!"

"And it's *my* house! When you're done respecting that fact, you can get the hell out."

Issac stormed into the kitchen where his mother washed the dishes. He huffed and puffed, waiting for her to acknowledge him. She did not. Finally, he gained his composure and spoke calmly.

"I'm leaving."

"Just be home before supper," Farah replied.

"No, I'm leaving for good. I'm not coming back."

Farah dropped the dish and rag and stood frozen by the sink.

"He stole my money," Issac continued, "My money! As if I don't give enough!"

"Well, I'm sure he had a good reason," Farah began, "Maybe he's getting the car fixed."

"He ain't getting no car fixed!" Issac huffed, "That damned car has died and gone to hell!"

Farah turned to stare at her son with a pained and bewildered expression. Issac was at first remorseful, but his anger soon returned.

He breathed heavily and waited for his mother's response, but she merely stood in the kitchen with her mouth open and a grimace upon her face. Looking at his mother, Issac felt a dull, aching guilt that he was abandoning her. Nevertheless, he returned to his room where he hurriedly filled a knapsack with his clothing. Just as he finished and turned to leave, he remembered his father's gun. He went to the chest by his bed and opened it. He dug past his charms— a music box, old photos, and old toys and books until he found it. He fingered the texture of the handle before he tucked it into his waistband. Then he looked about the room for a final time. Perhaps he was glad to leave it behind. He walked over to his bed and smoothed out the quilt. Then he turned and left the attic. When he got to the bottom of the lower stairwell, his father stood before him.

"You ain't taking anything out of this house," Abram declared.

"But these are mine!"

"And you are mine. I decide how you live until you decide you don't want to be here no more."

"I don't."

"Get the hell out, then."

Issac tossed the knapsack at his father's feet. He thought about the gun at his waist, and he trembled not to reach for it. With teary eyes, he looked longingly at his father and then past him, toward the door. He hurried out and down the main street. He turned left toward the station. He took the first train away.

§   §   §   §

Issac spent three years away from home. He worked in a garage in a neighboring town, and he spoke with his mother through letters in which she often implored him to come home. Only once was he led by familial nostalgia and longing to his old home, but he could not bring himself to enter or even knock on the door. He did not know what he would do if he saw his father, and he was afraid to see the grief on his mother's face. Perhaps he would see that his father's effect on her was all-consuming. Or perhaps he would find that it was he, himself, who had caused her anguish. When Issac finally returned to Moriah, he did so by a dire request that his mother would only discuss in person. Though, he had no desire to return, he felt that a vindication of the life he had sought and made for himself required that he resolve matters in Moriah once and for all. He was nineteen years old.

"How long?" he asked his mother when they had been seated at a diner not far from the house. "How long should one hold tightly to the stem of a dead rose before he learns that its beauty is gone and that its thorns merely seep the blood from him?"

"I don't know," she replied. Dark rings encircled her eyes, and the creases that had once been drawn at their corners now traced her sallow cheekbones and down-turned lips. Issac could not help but to stare at the the gray that had spread like clouds through her midnight hair. And, her voice had become raspy– a perpetual whisper, the flutter of broken wings.

"I suppose I had to leave alone, then," Issac said.

"And I understand why you had to go, but have you grown so cold?" Farah asked. "Your father needs you. You know what that house means to him. It's all he has left of his father."

"Maybe for that reason alone he should let it go," Issac said.

"Maybe," she admitted, "But sometimes people have a hard time letting go of things. It would break his heart to lose that house."

"Maybe it broke his heart to keep it. Maybe it will break mine further to help him keep it," Issac said.

"Still, you're the only person who can help him," Farah said. "That house is your birthright. It was meant to stay in the family."

"Like a ghost," Issac said reflectively.

"A ghost?" Farah asked.

"Yeah," Issac said. "Do you believe in ghosts?"

"I think so," Farah replied. "Something must happen to our souls when we die. Where'd that question come from?"

"I don't think I believe in ghosts. Maybe I did once, but not anymore."

"You're all grown up, then," she smiled weakly.

"I think so."

He paused for a long moment before continuing. "Tell dad I will buy the house."

Farah looked hopefully at him.

"Then you'll come home?" she asked.

"I won't," he replied. "Tell him I will buy the house, but he can't live in it."

"What a monstrous thing!" Farah declared.

"I disagree," Issac said. "I think it is the only thing I can do to help him."

"And what about me?" Farah asked.

"You should live in the house. Make sure he doesn't go back there. Make sure he doesn't hurt you anymore. I'll go to the house in a month. Tell him to have his affairs in order by then."

Thus it was that he reached the final step in the lower stairwell of his childhood home, and he answered the two questions he had asked himself when he first arrived.

"No."

His heart pounded in his chest, but his body did not tremble as the front door opened to his father's silhouette in the threshold. He let his eyes adjust to his father's face upon that shadow. Then, he thought of the gun at his waist, but he did not reach for it. He did not have to. Instead, he approached his father with the knapsack and tossed it at his feet.

"So this is your revenge, then?" Abram asked.

"No revenge," Issac replied. "There's no happiness in that. This is a pursuit— my pursuit of a happiness that I know exists out there somewhere."

Issac paused to pull his father's gun from his waistband.

"You wanted this to safeguard your fears. I will use it to safeguard my ideals. I think that it would be nice for you to find happiness. But you can't find it here."

Abram looked at his father's gun in his son's hand, and he felt a sudden but fleeting yearning. His own painful memories ran in his thoughts. He took a defiant step toward his son who quickly placed his finger on the gun's trigger. Both of their hearts raced.

Thump, thump.

He took another step forward and felt a strange nostalgia for son raising gun to father.

Thump, thump! Thump, thump!

He remembered, and he stopped. He looked at his son's scowl– so much like his. He tried to see a smile from long ago. He could not.

"Okay," Abram said resolutely, "Okay."

Abram reached forward and bent down to pick up the knapsack and sling it over his shoulder. Then he turned to look at the rusted sedan in the driveway. Issac watched his father become tired and old. Slowly, Abram shuffled down the crumbled path and toward the squeaky gate. He turned back to look at the house one last time before continuing past the houses he'd known all of his life. When he arrived at the main street, he turned right.

Issac returned to the house where he placed the gun on the kitchen counter. Then, he took a pen and paper and wrote a letter.

"Dear mama," he wrote, "I have sent misery away. Shoot him if he returns. Love always, Issac."

He placed the letter near the gun and walked through the hall and out the front door. He locked the door behind him and slid his key under the door. He stood tall and looked forward to the autumn canopies. There, he found a smile to wear past the gate, down the main street, and left, toward the station.

自由の夢

(Dream of Freedom)

自由だけでなく、
自由をよくわかって夢を見て。

Dream not simply of freedom but of freedom
well understood.

心のルーツ

(The Roots of the Mind)

良い思想の森にあなたの気を
植えて。

Plant your mind amidst
A forest of good ideas
And it will grow strong.

桜咲く

(To Bloom and Prosper)

思索して、
作を書く後桜咲く。

To bloom and prosper, one must not simply
dream it. One must create it.

蜻蛉の辛抱

(Calm and Perseverance)

蜻蛉取つには、
蜻蛉のように静止して。

To catch a dragonfly, one must become as still as
a dragonfly.

静かの雫

(Quiet Raindrops)

静かなうてきが落ちて池揺れ
つ。

The quiet raindrops
Fall into placid waters
To unsettle them.

A Flower's Bloom

My heart leapt in my chest
When my eyes met this flower,
Its leaves glistening
From an afternoon shower.

I thought I should be
Forevermore inspired
To behold its bloom—
A most radiant fire.

I acquired it at once,
And I so adored
That her beauty augmented
My chamber decor

My soul was uplifted,
And each day, it's restored
And thus, here's a promise
I shall never ignore:

Ma amour, if by chance
I find you neglected
Or left there to suffer
From my own transgressions

If I find you wilted,
Alone and distressed,

If your petals sulk,
Or your roots are affected,

I'll offer these letters,
As water to nourish
The roots and the flowers
I so dearly cherish
With hope that in time,
You will once again flourish,
And our souls together,
Uplifted. Refurbished.

A Yellow Flower Moment

"Is there anything more beautiful in its death than a felled tree?" Charlotte asked her son Sebastian as they sat on the front porch of his house overlooking the mountains.

"Try to keep still," he replied, "I can't paint if you keep moving."

Charlotte shifted in the wicker sofa by the porch banister and strained for a better look into her son's backyard.

"You know the expression, 'Take a picture; it'll last longer'?" she asked, her gaze fixed upon a dead and fallen oak trunk.

"I prefer the more artistic option," Sebastian responded.

"I prefer the option that lets me keep looking at that tree," Charlotte said, "Maybe lets me get up and walk around a bit while I still got time for that. I got plenty of time to be perfectly still."

Sebastian sighed and dropped his paintbrush on his easel.

"Mom, please."

"Okay, okay. Paint your picture. Just know that I think a walk through the yard would be just as nice."

Sebastian tried to hide a pained expression as he looked at his mother. Her frame was so frail and her legs so thin that she would labor to lift herself from that sofa, let alone walk across the backyard. He sniffed and rubbed his dry eyes against his sleeve. Then, he picked up his brush and resumed the portrait.

"Thank you," he said softly. Charlotte, however, continued to gaze pensively at the felled tree.

"Son," she said softly, "Are you having a yellow flower moment?"

Sebastian bristled at his distracted and distracting mother, and he let out an exasperated sigh.

"I thought you said you were going to let me work?" he replied.

"Do you remember," she continued, "when you were little and we used to walk to the park?"

"Maybe," Sebastian said impatiently as he tried to carefully stroke auburn creases into the burnt ochre skin on his canvas.

"I remember you used to pick the yellow flowers and take them home," Charlotte continued. "I would just laugh because you were so hard-headed. You thought you could do something to make them last forever. Do you remember?"

Sebastian did not reply, but he lowered his paintbrush begrudgingly to indulge his mother's reflections.

"Sometimes, you would barely step foot in that park before you would start picking them flowers out of the ground," Charlotte chuckled. "'I gotta use sugar in the water this time,' you used to say. 'They gonna die anyway,' I used to say. But you wouldn't listen. I think one time– only one time in the beginning, when your father went away, you sat with me and just enjoyed the flowers. You remember that?"

Sebastian closed his eyes and nodded. He took a deep breath, and became a small child again. He sat beside his mother and gazed at the bright yellow petals, each like little, frozen sunrays stretching forth from the ground. They seemed to radiate warmth into his mother's smile, warmth she seemed to desperately need, for she often shivered with the absence of her husband and the tears would lie frozen upon her cheeks. So, Sebastian would walk with his mother to the park, and he would admire those flowers for the warmth they gave his mother. And her tears did thaw. And her smile did endure for a while. Then, one day, they walked to the park, and Sebastian noticed that the flowers were not so yellow, and the petals sulked. And he feared his mother's tears would return.

"But I'm fine," she replied to her child, "I enjoyed them while they were here. Now it is time for them to go."

But, Sebastian did not listen. He tried to pick them and preserve them. He tried to close them in books. He tried to draw them from memory. He cried when he failed to recreate their vibrance with his pencils, and he vowed to be better.

He cried now, silent tears that his mother could not see because he dared not let them fall before her.

"I guess that is all for today," he said as he placed his palette below the easel and stood to help his mother from the wicker sofa at the edge of the porch. She clutched his arm with all of her strength, and he guided her through the house, the shortest path to his car in the front yard. As he drove her home, she sought to inspect him as she always did on their Saturday drives.

"You going to see your girlfriend today?" she asked.

"I don't have a girlfriend this week, either."

"Well, you should make one. You have plenty of opportunities with your work."

"My work is just that. The models come. I paint them. I don't confuse it with anything else."

"Surely, you've found a muse among them after all these years."

"As pretty subject for my canvas, of course. Nothing more."

"Then I see why you're so sad, sometimes."

"Thank you, mama. I'll handle my own affairs just fine."

"Of course, son."

They drove in silence until they arrived at her house. Then Charlotte remarked predictably,

"I know you don't believe in God, but you should come to church with me in the morning."

"We'll see," Sebastian replied as he always did though he had not been inside of a church in nearly twenty years. As he surrendered her to the nurses who guided her into her home, he knew that he had no intention of going this time, either.

When he returned to his home, he knew that someone was there, for the air had been unsettled by the unfamiliar scent of jasmine, and the carpets had been ruffled by light, bare footsteps whose whisper lingered into the anteroom. When he passed into this room, he was greeted by her voice.

"The is Sebastian's studio, yes?"

He looked briefly into her eyes, which looked directly into his, and he immediately knew to look elsewhere. He looked at her feet.

"This is Sebastian's home," he replied with no attempt to hide the irritation in his voice. "You must be Sophia."

"I don't know if I must be, but I am," she smirked. "You're late."

"I cannot be late to my house. You're intruding."

"I have an appointment."

"Yes. I was told you were an impertinent one, but that your beauty would make up for it. A presumptuous assumption, to be sure. It is rather rude to enter a person's home without his having invited you inside."

"Your key wasn't very hard to find. I assumed you wanted me to come inside. Besides, you're late."

"Very well," Sebastian sighed. "We have work to do. There is a changing room down the..."

As he spoke she began undressing in front of him.

"What are you doing?" Sebastian asked as he surveyed her body. He chose to fix his gaze on the delicate curve from her collarbone to her shoulder.

"This is a nude painting, yes?" Sophia asked.

"It is, but that doesn't mean—"

"Then what is the point of taking my clothes off in another room only to put on a robe to be removed in this room?"

"Because I do not paint in this room. But if you'd prefer to saunter about in the nude, don't let me stop you. I should suspect as much from someone who is missing her shoes. Come on, then."

He led her into the corridor where bright sunshine cascaded through the tall windows on one side. On the opposite side, were large portraits that he had done and that few but close friends and subjects were privileged to see.

"She's beautiful," Sophia remarked, "Any reason why she looks away in all of these photos?"

"In here," Sebastian gestured to the open door of his studio.

"Who is she?" Sophia asked. She had not taken her eyes off of the paintings on the wall.

"In here," Sebastian reiterated.

The doorway opened into a wide room with tall ceilings and immense glass windows on either side of the room. There was another door adjacent to the one through which they entered, and there was a large, empty, slate-colored wall opposite them. The studio was empty except for an easel and palette, a wide platform upon which sat a large ottoman, and a pile of empty canvases. Sophia walked over to the ottoman and lay across it in a graceful and serene pose.

"Is this what you want?" she asked.

"It will do."

Silently, Sebastian began sketching the contours of her body onto the canvas, his eyes perceiving all that he desired, his hand, all that it admired, and his ears, all that they required. He was even impervious to the fact that Sophia lay deathly silent.

When his sketch was done, he meticulously set about preparing his workspace. He lined each of his brushes so that each seemed perfectly perpendicular to the other. He applied each of the paints to his palette so that they were evenly spaced. Then, with quick swipes of his knife, he prepared his palette with skin tones, umber shades and almond hues. He chose his tools with the discerning eye of a surgeon. He traced the pigments around every curve and line until it seemed he had coaxed life from the still canvas. Her image transcended the page. Her body lay above the emptiness beneath her, almost as flawlessly as she lay before him as a still life on the ottoman. It was only when he was finished, when he was ready to speak himself, that he realized she had uttered no words through their entire session.

"I'm done," he said, and Sophia rose from her serene state and sauntered over to his canvas before he could give his usual objection. He allowed no model to view his work until it was in a gallery.

"Good," she said with satisfaction. She exited the room, into the corridor. Incensed by her further impertinence and by what he perceived as her irreverence for his work, he stood to follow her.

"They call you the "Soulless Painter," she said when she could hear his footsteps behind her.

"They?" he asked.

"The other models. Don't worry; we don't think your buyers are any the wiser," she turned to face him. He looked at her nose and wondered if even he could not sculpt a more perfect one.

"But apparently it is we models who are ignorant," she continued, "but not me. I know better. Now." She entered the anteroom and put on her clothing.

"Call my agency if you wish to book me again. It's been a pleasure," she turned to shake his hand, and he stood briefly with his mouth agape before quickly regaining his composure. He took her slender hand in his and replied with his usually austerity.

"I'll contact your agency if I require their services further."

But even he felt that his words rang hollow and redundant.

The next morning, he and his mother sat on his front porch again.

"You weren't at church on Sunday," she remarked.

"I'm sorry."

"I know. One day you'll visit me, I'm sure."

"Try to keep still. I'm trying to work."

"You know, it's not human to make people sit still for hours. Why couldn't you be a photographer? Maybe then we could walk through the yard like normal people."

"Some people manage to pull it off."

"Dead people?" Charlotte chuckled.

Sebastian winced.

"I had a new model here yesterday. She did a perfect job of sitting still and shutting up."

"Ah," Charlotte said, "So there is some kind of woman for you after all."

"A model that does her job?" Sebastian said. "Yes. I don't pay them to talk."

"Well, you aren't paying me at all, and I want to take a walk in the yard."

"You can't walk, mama," Sebastian said with immediate regret. He looked from the image on his canvas to the woman before him, and he wished he could blot out his mistake.

"Not alone," he tried. Charlotte allowed several silent moments to pass before she responded.

"I know." When their session was done, she spoke again.

"Just don't bring her any dead flowers."

When Sophia returned to his home, Sebastian was waiting for her.

"Does that make me special?" she asked from the threshold. "I was told the Soulless Painter never invites models back."

"It means you're competent," Sebastian replied while considering the strokes he would use to recreate her lips. "Most models don't know how to do their job.

"It's not too hard to sit there and look pretty," Sophia said.

"You'd be surprised," Sebastian said.

In his studio, the sun fell graciously through the window to kiss her, and she, with hands laid upon her thighs, head uplifted, and eyes closed, knelt before the window as if it were her alter. As Sebastian painted her, as the bristles caressed the canvas, he felt that he could feel her skin beneath his fingertips– the smoothness by her temples, the roundness of her cheek in his palm, the suppleness of her lower lip against the pad of his thumb. He leaned closer to the canvas to smell its toxic perfume. He admired the delicate nostrils and lashes as long as sun rays. He applied another stroke to her lips when suddenly he noticed it. A mistake. Alas! Had he inadvertently parted her lips? Did he beckon from her some utterance that might shatter the art between them? Quickly he painted her lips closed and looked up from his canvas to see if perhaps she had discerned his mistake. Yet, her eyes were closed. She was serene. And, Sebastian stared a bit too long. He wondered about her thoughts. He wondered how she could remain so perfectly still, so perfectly his work of art. He wondered if he were to abstain from making another stroke upon the canvas, would she remain this way, transfixed in bloom forever.

"I'm done," he said after a long while, and she opened her eyes and stood to walk over to him. He looked at the curve that implied her calf muscles behind her. She looked at the painting and smiled.

"Good."

He was afraid to follow her out.

The next morning, before the sun rose, he received a phone call and rushed to be by his mother's side.

"The Lord is good, isn't he?" she said when he arrived and she could hold his hand tightly.

"I wasn't ready for that call," he said past the lump in his throat.

"Me neither, son. But maybe today was almost a good day for painting," she chuckled. Sebastian forced a weak laugh. He fell asleep by her side just as dawn broke. He awoke to find her bed empty, and he found her on the front porch, seemingly staring at the bannister. He had to look closer to discover what she was really staring at.

"You know, I've been afraid of spiders my whole life," she said. "Really! My whole life, I'd jump up and scream and run into the other room."

"I remember," Sebastian said, "You used to make me kill them. One time you called me home from school to kill one. Remember that?"

Charlotte chuckled.

"Now, I don't know if it's just that I can't get up and run or what, but they don't seem so scary anymore."

Sebastian nodded as he watched the spider spin a web just a few feet from where his mother sat.

"You know what else?" Charlotte continued. "They make the most beautiful things!"

A single tear began to well in each of Sebastian's eyes, and he blinked them away while they were still mist.

"Let's go to church," he said.

"Oh, you don't have to do that."

"I want to."

"But you don't believe in that, do you? Or did you suddenly change your mind? Fancy that: me loving spiders and you believing in God."

"I don't," Sebastian said. "But you do."

Charlotte smiled.

"Finally letting those flowers loose, then?"

After church, they returned to his house.

"No more paintings, son," Charlotte said when they were on his back porch.

"Of course, not," Sebastian replied. He held out his arm and she wrapped both of her arms around it. Then together they slowly made their way down the stairs and into the backyard. They walked over the mossy terrain and stopped by the felled tree. She touched it gingerly as if to keep from disturbing it. Silently, they both marveled at the majestic gray its trunk had become. He fingered the grooves that had become a highway for ants that bustled to and fro. Charlotte looked at her son as he admired the insects. She discerned the solemnity in his eyes, and she spoke to it.

"Still having yellow flower moments, aren't you, son?"

He laughed weakly.

"I promise not to paint the dead tree, mama."

"That's not what I mean. Who is she?"

"He looked down at his mother, but for a moment he felt like a child again, looking up into her lucent, perceptive eyes, crying with a handful of dead flowers. He held out his arm to her again and led her into the house, down the corridor, and into his studio. He showed her his most recent paintings. She laughed.

"She has no eyes!" she laughed until she wept. "Or maybe she does. Who knows? They're closed in this one, and her back is to you in the other one. She may be beautiful, but how can I be sure? How can you even be sure if you won't paint her eyes? Have you seen them? Really looked at them?"

"I don't know."

Charlotte became serious and placed a hand on each of her son's shoulders.

"Son, you are a great painter. But you are terrible at being a human being. At some point, you have to stop being afraid to let things be what they are. Flowers die. Spiders scare. Love moves on. Sometimes there is pain in beauty. But your life is not made better for not indulging it in the moments when it can make you happy. Who knows? Maybe it'll make you happy forever after. One thing is for sure, it can only make you miserable forever if all you can find is the pain in it.

"I understand."

"Good. Then take me home. I have a friend to make on my front porch."

When Sophia stood at his threshold again, Sebastian looked into her eyes, and they stood transfixed for a moment, neither saying a word. She looked back at him with her most serious countenance and followed him to his studio.

"Aren't you going to remove your clothing?" he asked when she was behind her easel. She nodded and undressed. She sat on the ottoman with her hands laid simply by her sides. She looked directly at Sebastian, and he painted her. When he was done, she walked quietly over to him. She did not look at the painting. She simply leaned over to him. With neither a smirk nor a hint of irony in her voice, she whispered in his ear.

"Brilliant. Maybe next time you'll allow yourself to paint my thoughts."

Then she gathered her clothes and left his house.

The Unholy Spirit

Must I accept that my life is written
When I shall reject what I was given?
Whom shall I expect to determine my passage
When I must take steps? When I guide the
carriage?

What shall I render to he who purports
To provide my life and give it purpose--
My unyielding obedience, which keeps me still?
My judgment of torment and despair to his will?

I won't surrender my mind to a soul.
In heaven or earth, my will is my own.
I refuse to remain idly by and comply
So long as my feet can be moved by my mind.
I won't share the fate of my ancestors who all
          passed away awaiting blessings.
Verily I decline to submit my spirit it is its own
          sovereign, and my body with it.

A Forsaken Heart

Thou hath forsaken a trusting heart
Entrusted to you to keep apart
From blaspheme and evil that lurks in the dark
And words men conceive of as burdensome
      marks.

Thou hath forsaken an innocent soul
Entrusted to you for you to console.
If ever perturbed, your steadying hold
Should be there to right it, or so it was told.

Thou hath forsaken the unquestioned love
That children bestow with innocent trust
Expecting the same as if God above
Decreed their first breaths as reason enough.

Thou hath forsaken the one who must follow
      your knowing steps into the murky
      morrow,
For when it is weak, your strength it must
      borrow upon your song it looks to quell its
      sorrow.

Tears of a Native Son

I was born in the nostalgia of my mother's
autumn,
In a bitter-sweet moment, perhaps before the
dawn when
She heard a song rendered to her by the
meadowlarks, and
The wind whispered empty promises through
parting blossoms.

I was raised in the foreboding of my mother's
winter.
She cradled me against her ember soul those
cold Decembers,
For though her eyes were cool as coal, her heart
had burned to cinders.
Her sweet-bitter songs were lullabies that I
remember.

I was nurtured by the tears that rained in my
mother's spring,
And thus I dreamt that willows wept the pigment
in my skin.
Although I may indeed have been her joy that
dwelt within,
She never said the words, for love was but a
nigger's sin.

I learned to crawl, walk, and run during my
mother's summer
Amidst the storm torrents, lightning, and
menacing thunder.
Perhaps she feared that the world would break
my bones asunder,
But I would rather perish than leave my soul
encumbered.
I was born in the reality of my mother's hell.
What may become of my soul if therein I choose
to dwell?

Excerpts from In His Own Image
From Revelation to Exodus

The cool, dry earth has left the soles of my feet calloused and cracked. The crisp air has seeped all of the moisture from my skin. Gentle breezes are menacing hisses, and the sun does not shine for me but looms, an imminent doom, beyond the thick canopy of branches. I sit here in the shadows, coiled amongst the protruded roots of an old oak, my head tucked into the nook of its trunk, my knees drawn tightly to my chest. I wonder what it would be like to lie out there precariously admiring these waning moments of autumn. The moss would feel cool on my back where I instead feel the sting of dried leaves against tender keloids. I would seek the warmth of the sun rather than the cold of refuge. I would know intimately that ideal which I seek, that peace of mind that must come with the knowledge that each breath I take is mine.

My breaths now are measured and outwardly relaxed, but they are not mine. My father, whose whims gave rise to my being born into bondage, possesses them. It is to the great detriment of a man's mind and body that he be born a slave, but it is a much greater anguish on his mind if his enslaver is also his father. Mine is not an unusual case. As is evident by the many shades of brown that pepper the population of Howard County, slave owners are quite taken with the idea of increasing their property wantonly. If by chance a Fayette slave should look into a mirror, he might be haunted by the image. However, while many slaves in my condition may learn of their lineage through rumor or speculation, I am perhaps peculiar in that I know for sure: I am the son of Joachim Bishop.

Of course, though he is no more in the dark on this matter than I, he assured me often that our shared blood was of no consequence. I slept and awakened at his command; I ate what he saw fit to give me; I toiled for his benefit, and I lay exhausted by his ambitions. He declared through scripture and torture that I was his slave foremost. There were no places to which I could retreat for solace except my own thoughts, and even these were confined to my mind, never to breach the threshold of my mouth. My reason was stifled by the threat of the whip; my inquisitiveness dared not venture beyond the fields; my aspirations, though they manifested sparingly in my dreams, dared not linger there, for the dreams of a slave must dissipate with the morning fog, into the murky revelations of every dawn.

Every call to the fields was his declaration of my enslavement, so I declared my independence by escaping. However, I am just beginning the war. Though I rest now, I do so not by choice but necessity. If I should suddenly have to run, it will be by his provocation; every pant, every puff, and every gasp are his until I am assuredly out of his grasp. And further, when I cross into unsettled territory tonight, I will know that I have not yet shed the last vestiges of the slave to which he laid claim. My physical scars are not the only ones I carry with me on this journey. Though I will have endured the howls and the pursuit of his curs and withstood the curses from their tobacco stained mouths, though I will have eluded the jowls of wild beasts that would feast upon my flesh, though I will have staved off starvation, and though I will have freed my body from the possession of a man, I know that if I am to truly be free, it is my soul that I must salvage and liberate.

§   §   §   §

"Slave," he did not utter, "obey, in everything, your earthly master and do so for fear of the Lord." He glared at me through whiskey-glazed eyes, his jaw trembling from the force with which he kept his mouth shut.

"I shall bid my slave to be submissive to his master. And if he is not, he shall bear the punishment that must fall upon the disobedient," the words did not come forth from his mouth, yet they lingered in the air, it seemed, as the ghosts of past sermons. I only imagined that they might be words he would call upon now, for what other words might a father say to a son whose esteem he now sought to extinguish, whose soul he meant to extort from its body so that it might never again inspire such acts as mine had been found guilty of inspiring? What other words would be comforting for a man who had created such a hell for himself? What words, indeed, but those he deemed to be from heaven?

Though my arms were bound by ropes around the trunk of a sycamore, though all of my flesh was exposed to the autumn air, though my heart ached from the distant cries of a familiar voice, and my temple throbbed from the events that preceded my most unfortunate circumstance, I looked at my father, and I knew that his was the greater misfortune. I had spent many moments of my childhood contemplating that trauma of the flesh that the slave inevitably suffers for the sin of pride and ambition. However, on this day of reckoning, my mind was occupied by the sight of this pitiful creature, this man who himself seemed haunted by his own reflection. In me, he saw his broad shoulders slumped against the tree, his long legs hobbled by having been dragged through the woods, his jawline etched out in sweat and blood, and his fiery black eyes accented by that last glowering light of dusk— and by defiance. Naught but a few shades and a few decades stood between us. The rope that bound my hands was the cowhide that bound his. And when that cowhide tore through my flesh, he knew that his blood would be spilled.

He took one inebriated step forward, and I was immediately reminded of my mother's words from that morning.

"Hell," Miriam had said, "is earth. And men make it that way. They nurture it in their souls and carry it with them. They give birth to it in their words and grow it up in their acts." She had said this on a morning when the sun was shining, a cool breeze was finally stirring in the summer-scorched atmosphere, and the other slaves were dancing joyously about the quarters. The harvest had come in bountifully, and Joachim was in a generous mood. He had rewarded us with a holiday, given us new clothes, and even provided a barrel of bourbon, for he knew that the slaves would celebrate the harvest. And celebrate they did. Solomon told lively stories while the slave children giggled with delight. A few of the slave men stumbled about in a drunken stupor. A young girl named Serafina played a kissing game with some of the young boys while even some older men chased her around with groveling hands. My mother, however, sat brooding from the porch of our shanty.

"Fools always look happy," she grumbled while her nimble fingers turned reams of straw into baskets for next year's harvest. "You whip the smile into them, and then you liquor them up so it stays there."

It had become uncommon to witness my mother's smile. While the other slaves were keen to toast and make merry more often than not, Miriam had long ago resolved not to forget that happiness was but a fleeting moment in an otherwise miserable condition. While the other slaves sang Joachim's praises, she dwelled on the hell that he had brought forth and that they seemed to ignore. She glared at them when she reminded me that there was no salvation anywhere but in heaven.

"Good people are not made for this world," she warned me, "But if we just wait on the Lord..." She had uttered the beginning of that sentence often, but she had never finished it, choosing instead to trail off into a song. I rarely pondered her unfinished sentences, for I delighted in her singing. She smiled when she sang though her song was often somber. She sought salvation in the hymns, and sometimes she seemed to find it. She found it for me as well, for it did quell my own angst to see her happy-- if only briefly. Once, when I was but a young and foolish child, I thought that her songs of freedom were songs of her heart's desire. I told her that if freedom would make her happy, she should simply escape. She responded by striking me across the face with all of her strength.

"Don't ever breathe those words here," she hissed through clenched teeth, "Not to me. Not even to yourself. You hear me?" The pain in my cheeks impelled me to nod in obedience. She sang that particular song less frequently thenceforth, but the notion of sojourn grew with me. It started as a glimmer of curiosity illuminating a secret path of contemplation and ambition. What must it be like to be free? To come and go as I pleased? To discover the things that inspire happiness? To meet and converse with other free people? What do they talk about? What songs do they sing? What inspires them to dance? To work? Are they good people? And if they are, had they found some place on this earth?

Against my mother's wishes, I began to seek out Solomon's stories, for he often spoke about promised lands. I began to watch Goliath, our Negro foreman come and go by the master's permission, and I delighted in the rare occasions when I would be called upon to accompany him into town. I committed the routes to memory, while I searched the margins of the road, the plains that emerged from the woods, and the tall grass that hid the creek. Indeed, I searched the land for promises. I imagined what it would be like to run through those woods. I searched the faces of the townspeople to imagine their goodness and happiness. I tried to remember the scraps of conversations that found my ear. I remembered a song that a fiddler played outside of a tailor's shop. It later impressed upon me a wondrous dream of mellifluous laughter. Then on a night not more than two harvests ago, I found that my glimmering curiosity had grown fully into a luminescent desire to roam the world outside of my dreams and imagination.

It was a warm and humid night after a summer storm. The thunder still roared in the distance, so the slaves remained huddled in their quarters. It was as still as it had ever been and just as dark. The earth had been softened to clay, and I curled my toes in it. Then a cool and inviting breeze wafted by, enticing me to venture behind our little shanty. I took a deep breath and a few tentative steps. The moon peeked through the crawling clouds, but the black of the woods cloaked me. Slowly, I approached the crooked row of ash trees that separated Bishop Plantation from the rest of the world. The thunder cracked far in the distance, and I imagined the slaves huddling closer together in their barren rooms, each assuring the other that God's work was almost done.

My heart pounded, and I stepped into the world. The thunder sounded once more, but the world remained intact, I was sure, for the bullfrogs began to croak and the crickets began to creak and a hush of mesmerizing whispers beckoned me from the creek. I started to run as fast as my spindly legs could carry me. I ran, and my heart pounded, and the thick, warm air brushed my face and stuck in my lungs. As my heels displaced water from their puddles, my wiry arms swiped away the low hanging branches, and drops of freshly fallen rain fell into my eyes. Then the woods opened onto the high grass of the open plain, and there was nothing to hold me back. The air became a little cooler and my legs carried me so that I felt that I was flying. For a brief moment, I thought that I could comprehend freedom.

I closed my eyes and wondered if this was how the bluebirds felt when they swooped from branch to branch. I envied the wild horses that I had once seen galloping through the hills. Then as the hush of the creek grew louder, I opened my eyes and came to a stop. My chest heaved. The clouds had thinned, and the woods were far behind me. Here, in the pale gleam of the moon, I had begun to grasp fully the notion that the horses and birds were freer than I, as were the bullfrogs and crickets. How wretched was my condition that I was forbidden even the experiences and emotions of wild animals? After a long while of envying the flight of the blue bird and the galloping of the horses, I turned and headed back to the plantation. And as I approached the entrance to the woods, my heart stopped.

"Quincy?" Miriam's harsh whisper cut through the darkness, "Is that you?"

Before I had time to respond, her dark figure emerged before me. I felt the sting of her calloused palm as she struck me across my sweat-dampened cheek. I froze and made no sound. She struck me again before pulling me close to her bosom and holding me there tightly. Together, we silently stood amidst the whispers of the creek, the croak of the bullfrog, and the creak of the crickets. I felt that we would have made a tranquil scene but for the tremors of her sobbing. After a long while, she whispered again,

"You're a fool! You think you're all grown up, but you're just a big fool. If Joachim catches you, he'd— " she stopped abruptly, as if she had thought it better to put the words out of her mind, and she hastily dragged me back to the plantation.

That night, my mother cradled me as if she wished to turn my tall frame into the babe it once was, and she cried and pleaded. She rocked back and forth, and she sang every song in her memory. Then when she was weak from crying, and her voice was raspy from singing, she whispered,

"Don't make them take you away from me. You're all I have."

And my heart pounded in my chest because I wanted to say "Yes'm," and nod and be obedient the way that I had done when I was a child. But I knew that I was going to run again. The small glimpse of freedom that I had felt on that night birthed in me an insatiable desire to experience it again. I began to long for dark clouds and thunderstorms, for these were the setting of my happiness. Everyone, including my master, was preoccupied with their fears, and while they fantasized about God obliterating demons with each flash of lightning, and perhaps while they themselves hid from that obliteration, I reveled in the low rumbling bass of the thunder and danced amidst the staccato melody of the raindrops. Every flash of lightning was an epiphany of the life I began to dream for myself, and every calm breeze that quelled the woods once the storm passed was the briefest realization of that dream. Each time, I ventured a little farther, and lingered in my dreams a little longer. Then there was the night after the slaves had celebrated and a storm had come, when I ventured too far and indulged my dream for too long.

Reality crept upon me through the fog, first with the slight hint of burning tobacco in the air, and then with the low rumbling of galloping horses. Finally, I became alert to the barking dogs, but before I could consider an escape route, the voice of the slave foreman rang in my ears.

"Ooh, nigger you're in trouble, now!"

The rope wrapped tightly around my legs, and I was dragged the entire way back to the plantation. The ground, which had once cooled my feet, scoured my body. Twigs and fallen branches left splinters in my arms, and mud caked my eyes and nostrils. Finally, a large rock met with my head and ensured that I would remember no further details of my recapture. When I awoke, I could see my father off to the side, slumped as if he were exhausted or defeated. There stood a man before the mouth of hell and with no pretense.

"But he's your own flesh and blood!" the familiar voice cried out, and though this was perhaps meant as a deterrent to his actions, it instead served as a provocation. He stood tall and erect. A fire flashed in his eyes, his nostrils flared, and he raised the whip. I closed my eyes, and a blood-curdling scream ripped through the night air and clawed into my back. Every muscle in my body convulsed and my jaw clenched. I swallowed a cry, and just as that cry settled at the bottom of my stomach, her scream came again and tore down my spine. Lightning and thunder had converged and fallen upon me, and a crimson rain fell in torrents. I tried to remind myself to inhale, but each time, the air fought desperately to escape my lungs. I gulped several fleeting breaths before the scream and the strike came again. This time my head snapped back and my back arched. I panted, but I did not cry. The shrieks from behind me collapsed into helpless sobs but the strikes continued, lightning without thunder. My torso fought against the rigidity of the tree and my wrists dug into its bark. My breaths were out of my control, but my mind was opportunely blank; I would give no voice or thoughts to the breaths that escaped. After the tenth lash, my legs trembled beneath me. The earth fell away and the tree vanished. My last thought was that I had become a ghost; that my body had been taken from me.

§   §   §   §

I awoke several hours later and the memory of that evening's event flooded to me in one immediate sensation: searing pain that sent tremors through my body and tears to my eyes. I let out an agonized but resolute sob. Then I heard my mother singing as she applied a salve to my wounds.

"I got wings. You got wings."

I grimaced at her words, for they caused me as much pain as my wounds.

"All of God's children got wings," she drew out each note with a vibrato that turned the often jubilant song into a requiem. I grumbled and spit dirt as I struggled to turn my face from the ground.

"How can you sing those words?" I wanted to scream. "Look at me. Look at my back. All I have are lashes. Show me wings!"

Then I looked upon her face and what I saw frightened me more than the prospect of any whipping could. The face of the woman who had cried defiantly moments before and who had once looked upon the dancing slaves with self-righteous indignation was eerily vacant. It was as if she had wiped the previous hours from her memory.

"They're in heaven," she seemed to retort my unspoken words with a whisper and an empty smile. Then she continued with the song and salve. "When I go to heaven, gonna put on my wings, gonna fly all over God's heaven."

As she sang her song, I felt dawning in me a most important revelation. What all-graceful God would see fit to put men in a life such as this? What all-knowing God would give men dominion over other men? What all-powerful God would strike a man with such pain as I now felt, would smite a man for the audacity to dream of happiness? The audacity to know freedom? The audacity to think himself a man? What all-merciful God would make a man long for heaven at the price of living through hell? Though I had once regarded my mother's singing as a glance into heaven, I listened to it now and realized that it was no different from the sermons Joachim preached.

"Slave, be submissive for this is a virtue and the righteous path into the kingdom of heaven. Slave, obey your earthly master. Slave, fear him as you fear the Lord."

And as I thought of these words echoing about my nightmare by the sycamore, my body ached, not from my wounds but from my soul, which was stirring and becoming fully awake for the first time. And every part of it wanted to stretch my body erect against that sycamore, strain my wrists against my chains, direct my gaze into Joachim's eyes, and declare,

"I do not fear the Lord!"

Thus it was that while my father fancied himself God, and my mother sang his praises, I resolved to find heaven on earth. For six days thereafter, I learned to walk upright again. On the seventh day, I was sent back to work. On the eighth day, I took flight not merely to imagine my freedom for a fleeting moment, but to make my freedom real.

A Love That Consumes

I awaken to unexpected scents. I set a fire last night, two nights after the river had turned northward and I was presumably beyond the reach of bounty hunters. I looked forward to the morning when the aroma of its cinders would christen my freedom. Yet, I awaken to unexpected scents. There is the remnant smell of ashes, but it is overwhelmed by the stench of burnt tobacco, old whiskey, and stale sweat, scents that signal the presence of a stranger. My eyelids shoot open, and I scurry to my feet.

"Well, good morning," the words seep past stained teeth and an old pipe clenched between an inscrutable grin. A man in a long, dingy coat, worn corduroy breeches, and scuffed boots sits on his haunches with a rifle perched against his knee. The brim of his hat hides his eyes, and the match that he uses to light his pipe does little to illuminate his filthy, sun-scorched face. He draws a long breath through the pipe and expels a gray cloud. He wrinkles his nose from the sulfuric scent of the matches. He furrows his brow. Then, looking at me with mock sympathy, he offers me the pipe.

"You hungry?"

I do not respond, and my eyes narrow and dart about in search of an escape or a weapon. The heavily wooded area, which I had hoped would obscure my presence, now seems like a trap. Firs, ash trees, and birches stretch to the sky. Tall grass abounds, and there is but one path to the east that leads into the woods.

"No? Well you sure looks like it," he says, referring to my gaunt figure, the jagged shoulders, bony elbows, and angular knees that jut out from my own tattered clothing. He draws calmly from his pipe, never taking his eyes off of me.

"You know what else? You kind of look like you're not supposed to be here."

My eyes widen. I look at him with alarm, and he simpers at my expression.

"Oh, you have us all wrong, boy," he says, and I notice another man emerge on a horse amid the tall grass. "You see, we intends on helping you. We can give you a warm place to stay, some food to eat. And in return you can do a bit of work for us. Now, how does that sound?"

"I don't need your help," my voice is hoarse, but the words flow assertively from my mouth. I avert my stare from him to his partner, who is dismounting his horse. I find his dark, auburn skin and straight, black hair to be curious attributes, but the rope that he removes from the horse's saddle concerns me most.

"Oh, everybody needs a little help from time to time," the man continues while standing and emptying his pipe. Twigs snap beneath my feet as I slowly begin to retreat.

"He's fast, you know" the man proclaims suddenly and proudly. "I reckon it won't do you much good to run. You see, you may not need our help, but we need yours. And we sure intend to get it."

I dart eastward. His laughter rings behind me as I hasten into the woods. There is neither thunder nor lightning. Not raindrops, but evergreen needles fall into my eyes, snag at my tattered garments, and rake at my dry skin. Soon, I can hear the huffs of my Indian pursuer grow closer. When he descends upon me, I discover that I have neither the strength nor the energy to fight him off, and I tumble to the ground.

"Whoa boy," the bounty hunter hoots and hollers in the distance, "I told you he was fast!" The Indian binds my wrists quickly and drags me back to the fiendish smile and gangrenous teeth of his scoundrel partner.

"Tie him to the horse," he says, but as the Indian positions himself behind me to push me forward, I tuck my chin and bend forward slightly. When he tries to wrap his arm around my neck, I drive my head back into his jaw. I hear his teeth clattering together and a groan catching in his throat as I snatch my binding ropes from his loosened grip. Driven solely by the will to live, I scramble quickly to wrap the rope around his neck, but he ducks away from my clumsy lasso. I drive my bound fists into his back and try again. This time, the loop of rope catches in his gaping mouth, and I pull the loop closed, yanking his head backwards. He slumps forward as I jump onto his back. I have the advantage, but the scoundrel is approaching with whip in tow. He begins to whip both of us, opening several gashes in the Indian's shoulder before finally striking me in the back. I freeze from the pain, and the Indian is able to toss me to the ground and remove the rope from his mouth. The scoundrel aims his rifle at me.

"Now, I'd just hate to let a fine buck like you go to waste," he says through clenched teeth and short breaths. The Indian glares at me, the drawn blood forming veins down the sleeve of his shirt. With a loud "whoop," he starts toward me before a sudden, thunderous sound stops him cold. His eyes roll back and he collapses at my feet. A large, crimson circle begins to spread through the fibers of his shirt, joining the veins down his sleeve. The scoundrel looks aghast at the fresh corpse before his eyes dart about frantically in search of a gunman in the woods. We notice him at the same time, a slender but rugged man with squared shoulders. He emerges from the tall grass, his revolver aimed at the scoundrel. In an instant, the scoundrel swings his rifle, and in the next, he lies dead in the ashes of my first fire.

For a long while, I can hear only my heart pounding in my chest and the heave of my exhausted breaths. Finally, I look from the dead bodies to the gunman, and I am struck by what I see. His gaze is unwavering, his eyes like cold, grey stones. They are neither the shady eyes of the scoundrel nor the conflicted, angst-ridden eyes of my father. Nor are they the hardened, grief-stricken eyes of my mother. I have never seen eyes like these before, eyes that can look into mine with neither intimidation nor fear.

"You're going to die if you stay out here," he says in a sensible tone, and as if to signify that his words were a matter of fact, my entire body becomes limp. I slump to one knee, and my arms and legs tremble to hold up a body that has been emaciated by an arduous journey. The gunman hurries to my side.

"I don't need help," I mutter as he pushes a canteen of water to my lips. I drink voraciously.

"No," he responds quietly and seriously. "No, you don't."

He pauses for a long moment, studying me, perhaps.

"You won't make it out here," he reiterates.

"I've been out here for at least two fortnights," my words are raspy whispers, "They won't kill me. I won't let them."

"So I've seen. But I'm not worried about what they can do. I'm worried about what they have already done. I'm worried about what *you* will do to you."

Indeed, this man does look through to my soul, and perhaps he sees what I cannot yet comprehend. What has the world done to me? What acts has it made me capable of committing against myself? Of what has this man to concern himself in my regard? I am certain that I must revisit this topic again, but I am weak and weary. My belly is a void. My body is as light as a leaf, and yet I feel that I shall soon be unable to carry it. I crawl to a small, buried pile of berries and push a few of the shriveled bits into my mouth.

"You have made the toughest part of your journey," he begins. "I have some land not far from here. You may rest there."

"You will return me to slavery," I reply with a glare.

"I won't."

"How do I know?" I ask.

"The choice is yours."

"I won't belong to another man!" I yawp.

"I believe you."

He comes over and helps me to my feet. I mount the scoundrel's horse, and he mounts his own. He starts off without looking back. I muster all of my strength, and I follow him.

§   §   §   §

"It's easy for a man to believe in God; all that he requires is imagination. It is much harder, however, for him to believe in men," Winthrop speaks thoughtfully and seemingly to himself as we ride our horses at a trot across the plains. My energy has returned to me after a meal of bread, smoked pork, and whiskey. Winthrop had observed me curiously as I ate, and having seen my frail frame and voracious appetite, conceded the entire meal to me. He offered several reasons regarding why he did not need the food, but as I did not need persuading, I do not remember them now.

No longer distracted by my hunger pangs, I find his voice relaxing. Much of his meaning eludes me, and I am sure that we must revisit this topic again some day. But now, I am elated by the orgy of sensations that presently enwreathe me-- the song of the meadowlarks whistling in the distance, the cold breeze across my face, the fragrance of spruce and pine sap, and especially his voice, for his ramblings remind me of my encounters with Old Solomon, encounters that seem to have taken place a lifetime ago.

"You'd think that the opposite were true," Winthrop continues, "Sure, the proof of man is right there before one's eyes. But his soul is quite another matter indeed. Perhaps man is a myth, and there is no distinction between him and mere animals. Certainly, this would appear to be true when you witness some of the things that he does to other men. How can one believe in men, in the soul of men, when he so often shows that he is no different from animals?"

"I am not an animal," I reply firmly.

"Well, that is a peculiar assertion for a slave. A confident one, too."

"I am not a slave." I reply.

"Indeed, you aren't," he chuckles. "But tell me, what makes you so confident that you are not an animal?"

"I want to live," I reply.

"So do animals!" Winthrop exclaims with amusement, "Even a plant wants to live, I imagine." He pauses. "I suppose they'd say as much if they could speak."

"When I raise the scythe to cut them down, plants do not protest."

"Neither do men!" Winthrop is again excited and amused. I think for a moment.

"They can," I reply quietly.

"They don't. Not the lot of them. What are we to say about them, those men who would let themselves be cut down? And worse, what are we to say about the men who do the cutting?"

We ride in silence for a long moment.

"Are you a man?" I ask. Winthrop turns to look me in the eye.

"I hope so."

The wooded path clears, and the terrain becomes hilly. Long blades of grass move in waves against the wind, and rays of light break through the clouds to illuminate the play of wild hares and galloping mares.

"Come on," Winthrop shouts and speeds off. I kick my horse in its side and follow. The

107

cold air streams through the holes of my tattered garments and against my face, provoking tears from my eyes. Yet, I feel exhilarated. Never before have I experienced the role of master. As I guide the horse about the hills and around the bends of the winding paths, as I feel it yield to my unspoken commands, I become aware for the first time that I no longer toil with it as a beast of burden. I feel the horse beneath me; I look about me at a world that moves at my own beckoning; and I experience a new emotion. I feel that I can hold the world in the palm of my hand, that the winds are my own breaths, that the rivers are my blood, that the rains are my tears. I feel that the sunlight is my gaze and infinite capacity to know the world, that the clouds are my ignorance but that they shall soon disperse. As we approach the end of the path at the bottom of a hill, where a stream hurries across the terrain, I consider that I can become the mythical man about whom Winthrop previously inquired.

"What will I do on your land?" I ask him once we stop to rest.

"Well, you won't be a slave," he replies before kneeling at the brook to drink and wash his face. I notice that his hands and forearms are scarred and that his face is deeply tanned. His scars are like those of a field slave. So too are the muscles in his neck and shoulders. Strands of silver pepper his copper beard, and the slight wrinkles about his eyes and deep creases around his mouth belie the youthful leanness of his face. He dries off and smiles the most earnest smile I have ever seen.

"I suppose you'll heal," he adds.

"Heal from what?"

He folds his handkerchief and places it in his satchel.

"You're a fine rider," he ignores my question. "You learn anything else as a slave?"

"I can bring in a harvest."

"Good. A man ought to know something about how to feed himself. And he needs to know how to get around in the world. I'm sure there are quite a few other things he must know as well. But above all, he must know how to conquer this world. There are two very important skills for doing that, two skills I know particularly well. And I don't reckon you can become a whole man without knowing both of them. A man needs to know how to shoot. And a man needs to know how to read."

I wait for further explanation, but he says no other words for the remainder of our journey.

We rest, and then we ride in silence. I spend the time contemplating both the nature of a man and the nature of this particular man, who is unlike any I have encountered before.

§　　　§　　　§　　　§

I learned of my father's identity when I was a young child and fell ill. My body was stricken with fever; my sleep was restless and fitful; and my dreams were of an incomprehensible angst. For many days and nights, Miriam soothed me with cool, wet cloths for my forehead and a tranquil song for my ears. She calmed my soul such that I could ignore the troubled expressions that lay buried in her brow and pulled at the corners of her mouth. I awoke to her song, or I awoke to silence. Then one rainy night, I awoke to the image of Joachim seated in a rocking chair, staring over me like a spectre in the dark.

The creak of the old wood rang against the weathered walls of the cabin. The thick leather soles of his boots thumped against the earthen floor, muted and without rhythm. A rare fire warmed the room. It crackled softly, in contrast to the heavy raindrops that pattered in heavy thuds against the roof and windowpane, and it shone subtly on his cream-colored breeches and sodden, venous hands. The fire was, however, too dim to illuminate his face, and thus there was a void that spread from his chest, to the ceiling, and along the walls that the light of the fire could not reach. Were it not for his hands, those pale hands that grew whiter as he clutched the arms of the rocking chair, I would not have known him from a slave.

My heart leapt when I realized that he was he, and that he was not my mother. I was afraid of his presence, for I had never witnessed his visiting the slaves' quarters. I wondered if he could see that I was looking at him. I wondered if he was seeing me at all. He rocked slowly. The tips of his fingers glowed in the dim light. His foot thumped without rhythm. He said nothing. My fever grew hotter. My head ached unbearably. I returned to my restless sleep. I awoke clear-headed and without fever to sunshine, embers, and an empty chair.

I told Old Solomon of my visitor a few days later, for Solomon was, to me, the griot of good stories and unfathomable truths. I felt that mine was a good story and that he could make it comprehensible. Solomon did not disappoint. He deciphered the tale. He told me of Joachim and his infatuation with Miriam.

"The sun rose and a willow grows with the soul of an ebony tree," he began in his deep, mellifluous voice. "And the sunlight gleams from afar to admire what it sees. And it traverses from the horizon to its summit in the sky, its gaze all the while fixed upon the willow and her beauty.

He delights, does the sun, in his power to feed the willow. He longs to touch her leaves, her branches, her flowers.

"Now, the willow does weep, for it needs lots of water, and it longs to be by the unfettered current of the river. It grows, and it stretches its roots towards that river. But the sun, in his longing to touch the willow, reaches down and slowly dries the river. And the willow does droop and wither; her branches do bend hither and thither beneath the sun's lustful gaze. Then the sun retreats behind the horizon, where it will shine its dreams on the moon for the willow to see at night. And he courts her in the day and lusts after her in the night for the entirety of her spring.

"Then one summer, when the river is low and the willow is weeping, the sun ventures to touch her leaves, her branches, and her flowers. He kisses and gropes her with fervor, incandescent kisses and brimstone caresses. And the willow weeps; his desire for her is insatiable and unbearable. Though some fires are tranquil, and others do flare, though the caress of a fire is as light as the air, its fierceness is there; they all devour without care. By the autumn, the willow is all used up. Her flowers are gone. Her leaves have fallen. Her branches, once aflame, lie ashen.

"By the winter, the willow weeps often and bitterly. It never again blossoms in spring. However it does bare fruit." Solomon looked at me gravely. He held his arm up to mine to contrast his coal-black skin to my pecan-brown. "And the sun does shine brightly on that fruit."

With his story, Solomon had birthed in me a notion of my father's ominous omniscience. I had since conjured dreams of futile attempts to escape his gaze. On the first night of my escape, I had a particularly vivid one. As I stared through the darkness and dozed to imaginary images on the moon, a nightmare spoke to me:

"You cannot get away from me. So long as you have my eyes, I will never let you get away. I will search the ends of the Earth for you. I will never give you up. You will always be mine."

An Angel's Angst

"Ain't no use in you crying," her mother said to her on the eve of her departure. Miriam was at the dawn of her adult years, yet she did not wish to leave. Nevertheless, her master, old and hampered by debt, had sought and secured a satisfactory price for one of his last and most prized slaves. The buyer, Joachim Bishop, was a war hero whose keen business dealings made him a well-known and respected man in the town of Fayette.

"He a good, God-fearin' man. I reckon he be a good master," her mother was kneeling and trying her best to halt the flow of tears from Miriam's large chestnut eyes, tears that glittered on her dark skin like fragments of obsidian along the umber terrain of Cameroon. "I hear tell that he fancies you," she added in a hushed whisper while wiping the damp cheek with a coarse, calloused hand. Miriam cringed and withdrew from her mother's abrasive touch, and her mother grew impatient with her.

"You gonna have to learn to get along," she said sternly, "He can make it easy on you. Or he can make it mighty hard. God done seen fit to give you a good master and a better life than you had here. I just want to know that my own daughter won't suffer like I did. Don't I deserve that? Ain't I suffered enough?" With tears welling in her eyes, she reached for her daughter again. This time, Miriam did not have the heart to withdraw. She knew quite well how her mother had suffered, how her legs had grown crippled from the beatings she had endured, how her back had been lacerated with the brandings of a runaway. Miriam had watched the perpetual limp in her gait and the irremediable crook in her back, and she knew that the pain and distress in her mother's eyes were earnest.

"Promise," her mother pleaded, "Promise you'll survive, for me."

"Yes'm."

Her mother smiled a strained and solemn smile, perhaps like the one she would give on her deathbed when the pain was yet too much to bear, and death was the final relief.

"My, but you are beautiful," she said, leaning back to behold the sight of her daughter in the turquoise frock fashioned from her master's old drapes. Miriam was beautiful, indeed, for it seemed that a master sculptor had carved her entire body, her toned yet willowy arms and legs and her sylphlike waist, from the hardest and most lustrous ebony wood. Her cheekbones curved like baroque pearls, and her lips pouted forth like the soft petals of a gentian flower. Her hair, as black as raven feathers, streamed in thick, tight, untamed curls down a neck as long and graceful as a swan's. She stood there as a most awkward slave in a too elegant frock, its color providing a striking contrast against her dusky complexion. When Joachim came to claim her as his property on the following morning, he paused inadvertently at the parlor threshold.

Joachim gazed upon Miriam, and he experienced at once the most brilliant and the most dreadful sensations; the first melodies of an elegant sonata resounded and crashed into a cacophony of brash cymbals and staccato drumrolls; the sunlight broke into an iridescent display across a morning sky only to be covered by the cataracts of storm torrents; a scent like roses both enveloped him and restricted his sinuses; dove feathers seemed to caress until they chafed. His eyes tempted him with a wondrous oasis; his mind tortured him with the promise of desolate valleys and brimstone should he drink from it.

"She's all yours now. I suppose such dreams are over for me," the words of Benjamin Thomaston shook Joachim from his imaginings, and he turned to the stout and slumping figure that had appeared beside him.

"I beg your pardon?" Joachim replied curiously.

"Oh, I suppose there isn't anything wrong with dreaming," Thomaston continued reflectively. "But they do have a way of wearing on a man, dreams do. Mine have just about worn me to pieces," he paused a moment and then added with a flick of his wrist, "I'm speaking of course about living out my days as a rich slave-owner. I have failed in that endeavor, it seems."

"I see," Joachim replied.

"No. No, you don't see. You're looking, but you don't see."

"Looking?"

"Oh, I know the lookers when I see them," he said, turning from the slaves to Joachim. "I might not have all of the intuitions of you Southerners, but I know the lookers."

A spell of bewilderment passed through Joachim's brow.

"Oh, don't let me bother you," the man continued, waving his hand again to brush aside the topic. "I'm just an old crank, worn out by this Southern life. On to business, then!"

With a rapid but awkward shuffle, he led Joachim down the hall into the anteroom where he presented the bill of sale and they exchanged monies.

"It is a bit strange that you allow your slaves in the parlor," Joachim spoke with a glint of mockery in his eyes and the twitch of a sneer on his lips as he folded the bill of sale into his coat pocket. "Were it not for their skin color, one might have thought them your wife and daughter." The stout man's eyes narrowed at him for a moment, but then he assumed a somber expression.

"I have very little use for appearances these days. I have few slaves and fewer visitors. After Miriam, I have only her mother, and I imagine she is not long for this world. Perhaps I shall return to the north when she is gone."

"I could buy her, too," Joachim replied.

The stout man winced but looked away first, and Joachim did not notice.

"No, that won't do. She is a sickly thing these days. And besides, where would I be without her?" He looked at Joachim seriously. "Perhaps I do not understand the Southern sentimentality, but I do think, perhaps, that I can understand your attachment to this institution."

This time, it was Joachim who narrowed his eyes, and the stout man smiled wearily.

"You look. Soon enough, you will see."

Joachim felt uneasy as he left the house, and his uneasiness only increased when he walked past Miriam kneeling down in the back of his carriage. As he took the reins, he could hear the stout man shout after him.

"Get yourself a foreman soon enough. A good-looking young man like you should not be retrieving his own slaves. It's not good for his appearance!"

Those words lingered long after the plantation disappeared behind the carriage. The wheels clattered along the rock-strewn road, and the horses panted while their ironclad hooves kicked up dirt, yet these sounds failed to drown out the echo of Thomaston's speculations. Joachim felt threatened by his words, but he was not entirely sure why. He was also not sure why he was afraid to turn around, though he was acutely aware of Miriam's body in the wagon behind him. He kept his eyes fixed on the flowing manes of his horses. Their hooves beat against the dirt like an erratic pulse, and the wheels dragged across the rugged terrain like rattling teeth, and Thomaston's words rushed loudly into Joachim's mind, crashing against its walls with the seeming perpetuity of a tide against a beach front. Perhaps if he should look back and into Miriam's eyes, those words would suddenly become clear to him, and their reality would destroy him.

Miriam, meanwhile, sat quietly and appeared almost stately but for her slumped head and downward looking eyes. Shadows lurked where tears might have flowed had she allowed herself to feel something about her departure. The hooves beat against the earth, and the wheels chattered against the stones, yet her heart stood still, and her teeth were clenched. With each passing acre between her and her mother, she thought that she could bear it a little more. But she dared not look up at the quickly retreating path, and she dared not loosen her jaw. By sunset, when Joachim's carriage finally arrived at his plantation, Miriam thought that she had forgotten all of her past life.

As they turned from the main path and onto the stone-paved way to Bishop Plantation, the land that stretched out before them seemed perfectly serene with its immense yet well-manicured lawn and rows of ash trees, which seemed to have been lined and planted with mathematical precision. At the end of the paved way, just before the dirt road that led to the crops and slave quarters, a separate walkway ascended a hill upon which sat a regal house of late Georgian architecture. The pristine white of its wooden beams shone against the sunset and within the frame of its red brick quoins. The two chimneys on both of its ends stretched to the sky and gave the house a tall stature in spite of its width. The paneled, red door with its gold knocker completed the home's elegance.

"This is your home now," Joachim said in a voice that might have been considered solemn by Thomaston if he were there to hear it. Joachim did not look back at Miriam as he descended from the carriage and removed his gloves. A Negro woman with a plump, oval body emerged from the house, and a male Negro of slender build appeared at the side of the house, on the path where the cobblestone turned to dirt. Joachim handed his gloves and coat to the slave woman before speaking to the slave man.

"Make sure she finds her way comfortably," again he spoke without looking in her direction.

"Yessir!" said the slender slave, almost as one who was trying to hide his enthusiasm. Joachim and the housemaid disappeared behind the red door, and the slender Negro jumped onto the carriage.

"You're going to like it here," he said with a smile as he grabbed the reins and directed the horses onto the dirt path toward the slave quarters.

"Mr. Bishop ain't like other masters. He's a fair man. He treats us well." Miriam looked askance at him. There was something peculiar about him, something about the way he talked, the inflection in his voice.

The dirt path bisected the land, and even though the sun was sinking quickly, Miriam could discern the neatly lain rows of corn and wheat on the left. On the right, she could see the many tents of an immense tobacco field. Ahead, there was a large barn, and a large black pecan tree that spread its branches like a fan that caressed the roof. Adjacent to the barn were several small but sturdy wood cabins lined in a row. Smoke billowed from the chimneys of a few, and light flickered in their windows.

"That one belongs to Sarah and Zachariah," the Negro explained, pointing at one of the cabins, "They're a couple, and she is with child. That one there belongs to Moses and Beulah. They've been together since Mister Bishop was a child. They can't have children, but they raised him like he was their own. My name is Solomon. I have the little cabin there. There aren't many of us, but Mister Bishop thinks we can be efficient even though we are few."

It was the word "efficient" that made Miriam stare suddenly and with alarm at Solomon. She discovered what was making her uncomfortable about his words.

"You talk like white folk!"

Solomon brought the carriage to a stop at the barn and turned to beam at her.

"I'm a good student, aren't I? Mister Bishop taught me himself," he said with pride, "Most of us here can read. Nobody on the outside is really supposed to know, but Mister Bishop says we'll be better workers if we have a little bit of knowledge. I can count, too. I help take the inventory at the beginning and end of the harvests. I make sure the folks in town don't cheat with Mister Bishop's money. I bring him back his due amount every time."

He spoke proudly and Miriam stared at him incredulously.

"We have it good here. Maybe I could have earned my freedom by now if I had asked, but I figure there ain't much sense in that." He stopped and frowned in contemplation for a moment before continuing, "I have all the things that a free man can have but without all the troubles."

"But you ain't free!" Miriam said in a perplexed whisper.

"I'm as free as I need to be," he responded matter-of-factly. He undid the ropes around her wrists and smiled again. "You won't be needing these. You'll see. There's no better place to run to."

§   §   §   §

She awoke to his silhouette in the doorway. The sun shined a brilliant halo behind him, a halo that darkened him nearly to a mere shadow before her. She could discern no features but the teeth of his grin.

"The good Lord has seen fit to see you through the night!" he said with genuine excitement as he offered his hand to her. Hesitantly, she held her hand out to him, and he took it slowly and gently. He merely held it for a while, for she seemed reluctant to leave the corner in which she lay curled.

"You didn't sleep in your bed?" Solomon asked.

"It was too soft," she replied quietly.

"I see you fancy discomfort."

"I didn't think it was comfortable."

Solomon tossed his head back and let out a loud, boyish laugh that belied the gray slowly creeping into his beard and temples. His eyes glinted as he looked back at her.

"You are something else, aren't you? I'll bet they had goose feathers for you to sleep on at your last place, huh?" he was quite amused with himself, "Come, I'll show you the rest of the quarters."

The sun was rising radiantly over the horizon to display an idyllic land before Miriam's eyes. A pair of blue jays flittered playfully and twittered mellifluously by the apple orchards. A trio of squirrels in their chestnut colored coats and fleecy tails chased each other around the black pecan tree and along the mahogany walls of the barn. The field hands, dressed in ivory colored garments, worked diligently in the viridescent fields.

"Behold! The land of milk and honey," Solomon declared with a smirk, "Of course, we don't work with milk or honey, but still, we've done a good job with the place, don't you agree?"

"I'm sure Mister Bishop is good and happy."

Solomon did not catch the irony in her voice, and therefore responded enthusiastically,

"Indeed, he is!" He hurried her through the fields, introducing her with eager gesticulations, and the field hands smiled courteously before continuing with their work. Then he brought her back to the barn where he declared boastfully,

"These are my stables!" Holding her by the wrist, he led her to three of the four horses; the amber-colored horse was gone. Of the three that remained, one was a deep sepia color. Another was as black as midnight. And another was a rich golden color. All were well groomed; all had coats as smooth as velvet; and all seemed to stand with a majestic air.

"They're mine. Mister Bishop lets me be in charge of them, and they do what I tell them to do," Solomon beamed, and he let go of her wrist to pet and coddle the horses.

"I love these horses, and they love me. Ain't that right?" he spoke to the horses and seemed to briefly forget about Miriam. Then he looked at her again, smiled, and grabbed her wrist.

"Here, you pet it like this," he led her to the golden horse, and she withdrew a bit.

"I never been this close to a horse," she said.

"They're just like you and me," he replied, "Except they're more kind, more docile. I think we humans can learn some things from them."

She had begun to pet the animal, but she withdrew again when she heard him say the word "docile."

"What am I gonna do here?"

"You? Oh, I suspect you might work in the house. Mister Bishop went through a whole lot of trouble to get you here. He spent a lot of money, I think. But I'm sure you'll be worth it," he said the last sentence with his beaming smile and led her out of the barn.

"I'm supposed to introduce you to the housemaid. She'll teach you about you're work." He led her to the back door of the big house, and just before he let go of her hand, he said, "Maybe we'll see each other again. Maybe at noon." He appeared quite content with this notion, and he smiled once more before turning off toward the barn.

§   §   §   §

Each of the four rooms on the first floor of the Bishop house was the same square chamber, furnished elegantly but sparingly. In the parlor, a sofa, two chairs, and a small table lined two adjacent walls, and a piano sat near the heavily curtained windows. Three of the walls in the study were lined from top to bottom with bookshelves upon which sat multitudinous volumes. They ranged in topic from philosophy and religion to Greek, Latin, and the newest fiction from England. An oak wood desk and a rigid, oak wood chair sat in the middle of the room. A quill, a well of ink, and melting wax were set on the desk. In the middle of the dining room sat a long table of African rosewood with twelve matching chairs. A cabinet of the same wood stood in a corner between two windows with drawn curtains, and a few portraits hung on the walls. A chandelier of gilded wood and unburned candles hung from the ceiling. A light coat of dust veiled all but the table and one chair at its head. A few rays of sunshine pierced belligerently past the curtains.

As Miriam entered through the back door, she was struck by the darkness of the hallway, which ran through the middle of the house to the front door. The stairway, too, seemed to ascend into midnight even in the middle of the day. She was struck again by the brightness of the kitchen whose windows had no curtains and thus let in all of the light that shone on the plantation. Here, she met Esther, the housemaid, snapping green beans in a large wooden bowl. Esther stopped and looked up when Miriam entered the room.

"Well, I can see why he so happy," Esther remarked to no one in particular after looking Miriam over briefly. Returning to her green beans, Esther hummed in a gravelly voice a solemn song that she often hummed to herself, and Miriam stared quietly at her. Even seated, Esther was tall, and she had a portly figure. Her fingers were long, pointed, yet chubby, and her feet were swollen, scarred, and dry. Her walnut-colored skin was riddled with dark moles and deep creases, and her hazel eyes were cloudy. Nevertheless, the proportions of her facial features were such that Miriam thought she might have once been very pretty. Now, however, lines ran along her forehead and around her downturned mouth. Her pudgy face and fleshy neck hid any trace of a jaw, and her hair hung in thin grayish-brown tufts from beneath a knotted headscarf.

"I don't reckon Mister Bishop done brung you here to sit there and look pretty," Esther spoke with a tinge of bitterness, "This ain't yo' first day as a slave is it?"

"No, I just thought— " Miriam began, but Esther interrupted her with a voice that shook the silverware in the drawers and the dishes in the cupboards.

"No? Just 'no'? Well I never met me a more disrespectful nigger in my whole life," she boomed lividly, "I been on this here plantation since before even Mister Bishop was born. He may be master, but this here is my house. I been runnin' it all his life and half his papa's life, and I'll be damned if a little nigger child ain't gonna call me 'ma'am.'"

Miriam's eyes had grown wide with surprise, but she replied softly, "Yes, ma'am." Esther furrowed her brow and narrowed her eyes as she glared at Miriam with a deliberately drawn out silence.

"Well, I'm sure the Lord forgives you, but he don't forget nothing. You do right by me and we'll get along good, you hear?"

Miriam looked down and frowned, but she nodded.

"Good. Now, God done give you hands, didn't he? Use 'em to sweep that there floor. You can finish snapping these peas here when you finished. Then I'll show you the way Mister Bishop likes his linens did."

Remembering the words of her mother, Miriam walked quietly to the broom in the corner.

You're gonna have to learn to get along.

Indeed, she remembered her promise, but she tightened her grip around the handle of the broom as if it were a neck that she could wring. She was furious, for she loathed any encounter in which other slaves tried to assert authority over her. She began to sweep the ground furiously, but she quickly caught herself. Then she felt what she often did when she considered that nothing could be done about the injustice she perceived; she felt frenzied and hopeless. A sob stabbed at her throat, and she silently cursed herself for feeling anything at all.

Miriam finished every choir given her in resolute silence, and she did so in the efficient manner that made her Benjamin Thomaston's most prized slave. Esther could do naught but remain silent as she watched Miriam work. Every once in a while, she mumbled something about Miriam's being too thin, or she expressed surprise at Miriam's being able to lift a heavy load.

"I might have some use for you, yet," she remarked snidely once Miriam had refilled the supply of firewood in all three of the downstairs rooms, a job that was usually reserved for field hands.

"The real task is upstairs," Esther continued.

As they headed up the dark staircase, Miriam suddenly felt ill.

I hear tell that he fancies you.

She tried to remember what Esther had said earlier about someone being happy, and she wondered whom the old lady was referring to.

"I done had to send many little girls back to the fields on account of they don't do Mister Bishop's linens right," Esther interrupted her thoughts, "He very particular about his sheets and pillows. He likes them layered a certain way, and they always has to be clean." She opened a closet and shoved several folded sheets in Miriam's arms.

"Now you put these in there on the chair and then gather up the dirty linens."

Miriam carried the items through the door, but when she crossed the threshold, she froze.

"Child, get on in there. You act like you done seen a ghost," Esther chided her, but Miriam did not move. Her lips began to quiver and her arms began to tremble as if the linens were suddenly a tremendous weight.

"Child, what is wrong with you?"

"I don't want it," Miriam said slowly and softly.

"You don't want what? Lawd, the pretty nigger has preferences!"

But Miriam no longer seemed aware of Esther or her words. She just shook her head, her eyes fixed on the disheveled bed.

"I don't want it, I don't want it," she began to repeat over and over.

"Girl, get a hold of yourself. Here, give me the— " Esther reached for the linens but Miriam dropped them to the floor.

"I don't want it! I don't want it!" she began to bawl as tears flooded her eyes.

"Child, what done got into—"

"I don't want it!" Miriam shouted and ran from the room, tripping over the wooden threshold and landing curled on the floor outside the room. She rocked, and she sobbed, and she clutched her hair and temples.

"You gon' get the devil on both of us, you keep carrying on like that," Esther warned in a fearful whisper, but she had noticed Miriam staring at the bed, and her voice became a hush. She got on her knees by Esther's side.

"I don't want it," Miriam trembled and cried such that her voice became a tiny whistle, and Esther cradled her and stroked her hair.

"Ok, girl," Esther's voice became soothing, "Ok."

§   §   §   §

Esther finished up the bedroom alone, before showing Miriam a few of her bathroom chores and sending her outside to get some air. It was close to noon, and Solomon was waiting by the stairs of the back entrance. Miriam thought that he looked like an eager puppy.

"I know you're hungry," he said with a smile that irritated Miriam. "You didn't eat anything this morning. I know Beulah fixed us some chitterlings and cornbread. Might have some real pork meat, too. She sometimes cooks for us when Esther gets too busy. She's almost as good a cook as Esther, but nobody is better than Esther." He had reached for Miriam's hand again, but she held it away. He hardly noticed.

"You talk a lot," she said becoming annoyed.

"Well, I'm just happy you're here. I mean, we're all happy you're here."

"Esther don't seem none too happy."

"Oh, never mind her. She's never happy. But I can tell you she'll be glad to have some help in the house. Mister Bishop doesn't usually let many slaves in the house unless they're named Esther or unless they're bringing news and firewood. He especially doesn't like female slaves in there, but if you want to know what I think, I think it's really Esther who doesn't like 'em. She just chases 'em out of there. I hear she's afraid they'll harm Mister Bishop's Christian sensibilities. I don't think she needs to worry much, though. There ain't a white man alive more uptight about his Christian sensibilities than Mister Bishop," he stopped to laugh at his own cleverness, but Miriam continued toward her cabin.

"Hey, wait. The food is this way," Solomon called after her.

"I'm not hungry," she called back without turning around.

"You need to eat. I can bring you some."

"Don't," her tone was resolute, and her pace had quickened.

Solomon decided not to follow her but resolved to speak with her again later.

"She's just a little shaken by the newness of it all," he thought aloud, "She'll come around soon enough."

Miriam, however, would not come around. She was young, but she was not ignorant. She loathed being a slave, loathed being told what to do. And she was privy to the reason behind Joachim's desire to purchase her. She knew that he would come for her soon. In fact, when she heard the rustling footsteps outside of her cabin later that night, she thought that soon had come. The steps seemed hesitant at first, shuffling to her window and then her door before shuffling away and then returning. There was a quiet tapping at her door, and a muffled whisper came through.

"Miriam, you awake?"

She was surprised to hear Solomon at her door. She froze for a moment before crawling from her corner to answer.

"What do you want with me?" she asked through the sliver of an opening she had offered him in the doorway.

"I came to see you. I hadn't seen you since lunch time, and you didn't seem quite yourself then."

"How do you know who myself is? Why won't you let me be," she said irritated.

"I just wanted to check up on you. You ain't gonna leave me out here in the cold, are you?"

She opened the door wider but she herself slipped outside.

"I don't reckon you supposed to be around here this time of night," she said indignantly, though she kept her gaze down and her arms folded across her chest.

"Oh, I don't think Mister Bishop would care none. If he were here, in fact, I rather suspect he'd be quite happy with it." He placed his hands firmly on her shoulders and tried to draw her close. She immediately recoiled.

"What are you talking about?"

"Why, you and me of course. You've been running around in the house all day, and I ain't had time to talk with you," he ducked down to her eye level in an attempt to meet her gaze, but she merely looked away.

"I mean, it isn't official, yet" he continued, "but Mister Bishop done told me himself that— that you are for me," he wanted to speak assuredly, but his courage was leaving him.

Miriam backed up slowly until her heels and shoulder blades were pressed against the door.

"I'm the only one here that doesn't have someone for himself. Mister Bishop says it'd be good for me to settle in and have a family. He said he'd find me a good wen— a good woman. And here you are!" she could see his nervous smile by the light of the moon, and she closed her eyes tightly to blot it out of her mind. He continued, "I couldn't never dreamed you'd be so pretty, but here you are, like an angel, and—," but Miriam heard enough and cut him off.

"What if I don't want you?" she blurted out.

"I—I," he stammered.

"What if I want someone else? What if I don't want nobody?" she could feel the sting return to her throat, and she tried to hold her tears tight in her clenched eyelids.

"I—well," he stammered, "Well, that's not how things work. I mean— you are mine. And— and I am yours. If Mister Bishop says—," he searched hard for his words, but they wouldn't come out the way he wanted them to.

"What if I'd rather die?" she spat these words at him in the hope that he would retreat.

"Now you just trying to hurt my pride, girl. You'll see. I—I'm a good man!"

"I ain't never met one of those, and if I ever do, I know he won't be no slave!" she hurled the words at him like daggers, and they worked, for he stopped searching for her with words and instead sought her with his hands. But her own hands had found the door latch, and she quickly escaped inside.

§   §   §   §

It was once a great source of pride for the slaves on Bishop Plantation that none of them had ever been whipped. Though it always loomed over them as a possible punishment, there wasn't a slave among them who had dared to commit the act worthy of that punishment. Indeed it was only a slave's attempt to escape slavery that led to whipping, for in matters of work, Bishop was a peculiar master; he did not believe in ruling by physical force.

"I make use of mental confines, for it has been my experience that fear of the cowhide inspires not great work but merely completed work," he once explained to a group of eager listeners at a dinner party in Springfield. They were slave owners and pro-slavery sympathizers from various parts of the country. They were bankers and doctors, pastors and slave hunters. Even a particularly shrewd businesswoman looked on attentively. They all wanted to know the secrets to the overwhelming prosperity at Bishop Plantation.

"A slave has to feel empowered, however illusory that feeling may be."

"So you empower your slaves?" the pastor stepped forward to respond with a tone of derision.

"With limitations of course, for what is a slave without limits," he laughed and his guests laughed nervously with him. "No. I endear him to me. You see, fear makes the slave anxious and miserable, eager to change his station in life. Such sentiments in a slave require the constant aim of a gun to his head if it is to be held at bay. And trust me gentlemen, nothing is worse for business than a dead or maimed nigger."

"Well how do you keep them from escaping?" asked another.

"Ah, but the reverence and loyalty of a slave knows no bounds. And freedom is but a trifling thing to he who can see naught but the benefits of slavery. Treat your slaves rightly and justly, as the Lord sayeth, and he will be like the slave in Exodus who would declare 'I love my master; I shall not go free.'"

"Then you employ the Word of our God," the pastor replied with a nod of approval.

"But of course! What greater authority shall a man appeal to if not his?" Joachim assured him.

Thus it had always appeared that Bishop was a prophet, for his slaves often bragged to the slaves of other plantations about the riches they shared at Bishop Plantation. They bragged with their words, and they reveled in the chance to show off their healthy, unscarred bodies. They knew how to behave to avoid the whip, and they never expected to see anyone among them maimed. They were therefore awe-struck on the morning when Joachim returned to the plantation with a new slave that bled profusely from each of his bandaged feet and hands.

"Solomon!" Joachim shouted from the cobblestone path, "Come get this nigger before he bleeds to death in the damned carriage!"

Solomon would one day tell everyone the tale of how Joachim Bishop was attacked by his new slave foreman before beating him into submission with his own bare hands and shooting him to keep him subdued. However, that day, the slaves would only stare dumbfounded as Solomon tried to carry a broad-chested, goliath-like Negro into the barn.

That morning was also the first day that Miriam had seen Joachim since her arrival. Until then, she had helped Esther tend to the house quietly, and her episode in his bedroom was nearly forgotten. Esther had returned to her severe tone, and Solomon had continued to court her. Perhaps he had started to wear on her, too, for she smiled once or twice during that week. She had also stopped contemplating escape, but this had little to do with Solomon. On one evening, when a doughty spirit had caught hold of her and led her past the crooked row of ash trees, trepidation seized her by the throat and dragged her back to the plantation. When the moon seemed to serve as a beacon toward the possible, the clouds gathered to shroud her resolve with the absoluteness of the impossible. The air, at first crisp with the clarity of opportunity, began to swirl with a wind that howled like circling hounds about her. Her dream of what life ought to be was overwhelmed by the reality of what life was. And that reality was inescapable. Thus, when Solomon caught her staring wistfully past those trees one day and thought to tell her a tale that would still her, he was unaware that she had already stilled herself.

"I once seen him shoot the eye out of an eagle's head when it was way up in the sky," he boasted of Joachim, "and in the war, I've heard about how he hunted down the redskins on their own land and brought their heads back to his general. He wasn't much older than you are, now.

Nope, I don't think it would take him too long to find a man if he really wanted to get him."

With some remnant of doughtiness left in her, Miriam scoffed at his tales, but in truth, her imagination was wholly captured. She convinced herself that she was keeping her promise to her mother, and she stopped looking past those trees. She learned her chores, and she did them well and peaceably. And on that day, when a goliath had to be dragged into the barn, and Joachim walked about the house noticeably perturbed by whatever encounter had caused that goliath to stain the dirt road along a slaves' green paradise, she tried her best to tip-toe through the house like a ghost. She worked quickly when she had to be upstairs, and she sought not to be caught alone with him in a room. She did not succeed.

"I hope you're finding your way here well enough," his deep voice sounded from behind her in the study, and her heart nearly jumped out of her chest. She had been dusting the bookshelves when she made the mistake of examining one of the books out of curiosity. Solomon had piqued her intrigue when he once likened her to a character in a story he had stolen from this library; not every book was permissible to the slaves.

She held the book firmly and smelled the musk of its old pages. She caressed its leather skin and embroidered spine, and though she could not read the title, she wondered if she would find the woman that was like her on its pages. She dropped the book quickly and shamefully when she heard Joachim's voice.

"Yes, sir," she replied with her head bowed. Her shame caused her to lie, "I do like it here."

"Good," he said with a wry smile, "Please, continue." he walked over and retrieved the book from the floor. He handed it to her. "Do you know what's in these?"

"No, sir."

"The whole of human knowledge," he said gravely before donning a smile that contradicted the look in his eyes, "but I don't expect you to understand that." He turned and walked away from her, and she was glad, for she did not like the solemnity of his gaze.

"You can learn to read that, if you'd like," he continued as he walked over to the shelf farthest from the window, "Many of my Negros here can read. Some of the older ones choose not to, and that's fine, I suppose. You can't force someone to use his mind." He paused. Away from the light of the window, one would have missed the subtle look of doubt that his own words summoned to his face. One would have also missed how he gazed at Miriam while she held the book, how he envied the sun's rays which seemed more persistent than ever as they rushed past the curtains to fall upon her slender shoulders and caress the subtle hints that her dress gave of her collarbone. He gestured soberly to wipe away his thoughts, and he tried to chuckle lightly.

"I think I'd like to learn," Miriam spoke quietly, starring at the book in her hands.

"It's settled then," he declared seriously, "You'll find that Solomon is a good teacher. I taught him myself."

Miriam thought she heard a trace of pride in his voice, but his countenance was austere.

"Don't tarry here long. I have work to attend to."

That evening, Joachim called Solomon to his study.

"She'll be your student," Joachim stated, his eyes peering from behind a heavy volume and over the gold brim of his reading glasses. A wide, toothy grin spread across Solomon's face.

"Thank you, master! I'll teach her good, and—,"

"Well." Joachim interrupted him.

"I'm sorry, sir?"

"You'll teach her well, and that's all you'll do."

"I don't understand," his ignorance froze the smile onto his face.

"Of course you don't, Solomon," he closed the volume and placed it heavily on the desk, "You are to teach her, but you are not to touch her."

"I beg your pardon, master. I thought you had gifted her to me."

"I haven't."

The smile melted from Solomon's face.

"To be my wife."

"I did not."

"Master, if it pleases you, I'd very much like her—,"

"It does not."

Joachim picked up the book and opened it again, signaling an end to the discussion. Solomon stood, his mouth moving with no words coming out of it.

"That will be all, Solomon. You'll start tomorrow after the morning work."

Solomon felt a great stinging in his eyes and throat and a tingling in his fingers. He was paralyzed both in body and spirit, and though he felt the urge to say something else, he knew that he dared not. Swallowing hard, he turned and left the study. Down the dark hall, he walked with heavy steps; past the kitchen, he heard a solemn song in a gravelly hum. Out the back door, a chill stirred his long-slumbering soul; down the dirt path, his burden grew palpable and inexorable. In the moonlight, his pride was revealed to be a façade; toward the crooked ash trees, his vision grew blurry. Under his breath, he cursed Joachim; by some vestigial pride, he thought to escape. On that night, he returned to his quarters; at sunrise, he returned to his work.

§   §   §   §

Miriam slept fitfully on those first days on Bishop Plantation. The breeze awakened her when it knocked at her door, and the moonlight did, too, when it peered through her window. Raccoons and gophers crept through the dried leaves outside and stole the solace from her dreams.

"What are these footsteps that I hear?" she shouted at baleful shadows. "Who looks through my window? Who haunts me from behind that door? What do you wish to take from me? Please tell me, I implore!

"Why do you torture me in sleep? How shall I rest in peace? Should I submit to hell's embrace? For yet, he'll come for me.

"If I should yield the monster's grasp and kisses from demons, no howls from wolves, nor hiss from asps shall stir my sweet dreaming.

"What can you take when I'm awake, if I bequeath this realm? If I profess to love no thing, no man can steal the song I sing. By none shall I be overwhelmed. My soul shall some day soar!"

At once, she awakened in the still of the night, and there he stood at her opened door. The moon shone a crown above his head, and his figure pervaded the room with the shadows. She closed her eyes again, breathed calmly and deeply, and embraced the darkness.

Made in the USA
San Bernardino, CA
14 February 2018